LISA HELEN GRAY

MASON

CARTER BROTHERS SERIES: BOOK TWO

CONTENTS

All our dreams can come true;
if we have the courage to pursue them.
Walt Disney

CONTENTS

PROLOGUE

DENNY

Giving my room one more glance over, I make sure I haven't forgotten anything, and sadness engulfs me. All my bags are packed, and Nan is waiting for me downstairs. There's nothing left for me here.

My parents don't want me. *He* doesn't want me. And I'm pretty sure this is how my life is going to be for the rest of my days.

No one is ever going to want me.

For eighteen years, I have tried to make my parents proud, but nothing I did was ever good enough. My news yesterday only confirmed what a disappointment I really am to them. It's why I'm leaving with my nan to live miles away from here.

My life really sucks.

"Are you ready, Denny?" Nan asks, sneaking up on me. Not even the bangles on her wrist alert me to her arrival.

"Is it okay if I say goodbye to my friends before we leave?"

"Of course, you can. I'm going to visit an old friend and say goodbye whilst you do that. Call me once you've finished and I'll pick you up. Is that okay?"

"Sounds great," I lie.

I don't want to go, but it's the best thing for me right now. I need a fresh start, and my nan is willing to help me with that.

She leads me down the stairs, to where my parents are. My mother is standing by the grand marble fireplace, looking beet-red in the face as she speaks in a low tone to my father. He's sitting down in the armchair like a schoolboy getting told off by his teacher. That's the thing about my dad; he doesn't have a backbone where my mother is concerned. She says jump; he asks how high. It's always been the same. God forbid he ever has an opinion.

"We're off, Charles. Denny is going to say goodbye to her friends, so I'll go visit with Deborah."

"That sounds—" my father starts.

"Like a bad idea," Mum interrupts, her expression stone cold, void of any sort of emotion or remorse for the things she said to me earlier. "After all, those friends of yours are to blame for corrupting you. You will do no such thing. You will stay here and *fix* your mistake."

By fix, she means abort.

"Well then, Vivian, it's a good job she isn't in your care anymore, isn't it?" Nan retorts sharply.

I duck my head, my lips twitching. Nan hates my mum as much as I do, and isn't afraid to let her know just how much.

We live in what people call the richest part of town, where the houses are bigger and the people are stuck up. Most of them are anyway. My mother just seems to be the worst. Heaven forbid someone answer her back. Though, seeing her expression at being talked back to is amusing.

"Charles and I have agreed that Denny living with you is a bad idea. It doesn't seem like a punishment. After all, it's time Denny finds her own way—if she isn't going to deal with the problem."

"Well, *Vivian,* you don't get to decide. Denny turned eighteen last week, so legally, she is free to do as she pleases."

My nan really does kick ass when she gets going!

"Don't be absurd. She doesn't turn eighteen until next week. I should know; I'm the one who gave birth to her," Mum snarls, her lips twisting in disgust.

"Yes, you should know," Nan replies bitterly.

Mum opens her mouth to speak, but I interrupt her. I don't want to drag this out any longer. I want to visit Harlow before I leave. She's expecting me. When I finished packing the last bag, I sent her a text message to ask if it was okay to go over. She replied with a '*Hell yes!*'.

I step further into the room instead of standing in the background like I always do. "It was last week, Mum. You would know if you ever paid any attention to me," I snap, feeling brave.

I'm just done with being walked all over. I'm so angry at them, but I'm disappointed in my dad more than anything. He just stood there and let my mum say all those cruel things about me. He was supposed to be on my side, and yet he said nothing.

"Don't talk back to me, young lady," she snaps.

"Someone needs to," I retort, giving my dad a pointed look. He ducks his head, unable to look at me.

Mum sucks in a breath, flabbergasted. "You're still young enough to get a spanking."

"And I'm old enough to slap you back. I'm done being scared of you. You can't control or hurt me anymore."

"Get out of my house! Right now. I'll not have you insulting me in my own home," she yells.

Dad looks up at me, his expression downcast. He opens his mouth, and a spark of hope hits me. I want him to stand up to my mother, to stand up for himself and for me.

And just when I think he'll do the right thing, Mum moves over to where he's sat in the chair and squeezes his shoulder.

His gaze drops to his lap, and all hope flies out of the window.

"Goodbye, Dad," I tell him quietly.

My nan tuts in disgust before helping me carry the last of my luggage to the car. I can't risk leaving anything here. The minute I shut the front door, I know she'll have people on the phone ready to come and strip what is left of my things. It will be like I was never here. And I don't care. Everything important or sentimental is coming with me. The few things I have to leave mean nothing. She can burn it for all I care.

With one last look inside the house I grew up in, I inwardly say goodbye to my old life.

Because I'm never coming back here.

———

L ying down on Harlow's bed, I run my finger over her blanket, trying to find the words I need to say. I'm scared that once I say them out loud, it's going to be real, and right now, I'm happy to pretend it isn't.

I just don't know how to say goodbye to the girl who changed my life. She's my best friend, and I love her. But as much as I want to stay, to support her—I can't be here with *him* next door, knowing he's got another woman there.

I can't. Not after I tried to talk to him one last time, only to be greeted by another woman he was occupying his time with. My heart broke a little more, and the last bit of hope I had clung to, went away. I didn't wait for him to come to the door before escaping to Harlow's.

I can't embarrass myself anymore when it comes to him. I've done it enough, and I am done.

Now here I am, wasting my last moments talking about nonsense when I should be telling her goodbye, and explaining the reasons as to why I'm leaving.

Harlow's phone vibrates from her desk, and a goofy grin spreads over her face when she looks down at the screen.

I don't need to ask who it is, but I do anyway. "Malik?"

She nods, and answers the phone. Her eyes sparkle, taking on a dreamy look when he replies. I can't hear their conversation, but I don't need to. I can see how happy she is at just hearing his voice. I wish I had that. I *want* that.

Malik—Harlow's boyfriend—has been there for her since she walked into class on her first day. I'm happy she has him. He stuck by her through all of her trauma, and made her smile again. But as happy as I am for her, I'm also jealous as hell.

She has a guy who didn't run when things got serious, who protected her and her feelings, whilst being faithful to her as she was to him. Even tonight, he was reluctant to leave her side. I think something he saw in me when I first arrived made him take a swift exit. He must have sensed I wanted to talk to her without him around and knew it was important. Otherwise, he wouldn't have left.

I want that. I want someone who will shield me from evil, who will protect me from my parents and those who mean to cause me harm. I want someone who will hold me when times get hard and assure me everything will be okay, like I needed when I found out I was pregnant. I want someone to love me, and let me love them in return.

Snapping out of my thoughts, I catch the last part of their conversation, my ears perking up.

"See you soon," she tells him, ending the call.

I pull in a breath, knowing this is the time to tell her. I can't put it off any longer, not when we have a three-hour car journey to make and it's getting late.

When she continues to stare down at her phone, I ask, "Is everything okay?"

She jumps, startled. "Yeah. I think. That was Malik. He sounded weird."

"Weird how?"

She shrugs. "I'm not sure. He said Mr. Gunner has found a way to help me move on. He wants me to meet him at the old Gunner house. Will you come with me?"

I glance down at my watch, wishing I had more time. I grab my phone and send out a text to my nan.

DENNY: Hi Nan, I've just got to do something with Harlow. I'll meet you on the back road by the bus stop, near the old Gunner house.

NAN: Okay, sweetie. I know this is hard for you to do, sweetheart, but it's not going to get any easier.

DENNY: I know. See you soon. X

I glance up from my phone, forcing a smile. "Yeah, I can come. I'm kind of intrigued as to what he wants. I can't stay for long though. I have to go somewhere with my nan."

"Is everything okay, Denny? You said you needed to talk, but you've avoided any conversation since you got here. You're starting to worry me."

I duck my head when tears threaten. "There is something I need to talk to you about, but it can wait. I'll tell you once we know what Malik wants."

"Are you sure? I can call him back and tell him no."

I force another smile, grabbing my jacket off the bed. "Nope. C'mon. Let's go see what he wants."

She reluctantly grabs her coat too. "Okay. But promise me you'll talk after."

"I will."

———

The taxi pulls up outside the old dirt road that leads to the Gunner house. Malik is waiting on the other side of the fence that's blocking any cars from going up. He has the biggest grin on his face, which is a feat for someone who is always brooding. Clearly, whatever he wants to show her is important, not only because he's grinning, but because I know he'd never bring Harlow back here if there wasn't a good reason. Too much happened here.

She hands the taxi driver his money before stepping out of the car. I follow, taking her lead when she heads for the gate.

"This better be good," Harlow warns him as she fiddles with the cuffs on her coat.

He helps her over the fence. "You'll be fine, babe. I wouldn't bring you out here if I didn't think this may do you some good," he explains.

"Is that smoke?" I gasp when he starts to help me over.

The smell of smoke is strong in the air as we walk towards the old house. I grin when we get near, seeing the old house burning to the ground. It's about time someone did this.

"Did you do this?" Harlow asks, her tone concerned but laced with awe.

I turn to hear his reply, but a man I recognise as Chris's dad catches my attention. He's marching over in our direction, his expression grim.

Uh-oh.

"No, it was my idea," Mr Gunner answers, taking me by surprise.

It's a relief to hear they aren't going to get arrested for burning the house down. Still, I'm sure inhaling the fumes isn't good for me or the—

I close my eyes. I can't even say it.

Walking further from the house, I lean against a fence, watching as the flames engulf the old home.

My phone vibrates, and I pull it from my pocket. It's a message from my nan. She's waiting for me down the road. I need to get this over with, but seeing Harlow wrapped up in Malik's arms, crying with joy, I don't want to ruin the moment.

When I see Hannah, the bitch who caused Harlow nothing but pain, making her way over to Harlow, my jaw locks. The cow really has a nerve.

I push away from the fence, about to intervene, when she spots me and stops in her tracks for a moment. It doesn't stop her from going over to them, clearly forgetting I'm not scared to hit back. She learnt that lesson a few weeks ago when I punched her in the face. I'm about to go after her, to get her to leave them be, when I spot Mason over by the wall, chatting with the rest of his brothers.

I jerk to a stop when I see he's not alone. The wind is knocked from my chest, and I struggle to swallow past the lump in my throat at the sight of the girl hanging off his arm.

Tears gather in my eyes when I notice it's not even the same girl who answered his door earlier. It's a new one.

And this is what it will always be like. Why I need to get out of

Coldenshire. There is no way I can handle seeing him with someone new every day whilst I have his baby growing inside of me.

Sensing eyes on him, he scans the area, his gaze coming to a stop when he spots me. I swear he can reach inside of my soul with just one look; can read all my thoughts and desires. His chocolate brown eyes dilate, turning into a darker shade, much like they do when he's angry or turned on.

I looked into those eyes and felt love reflecting back at me.

Or so I had thought.

It was all a lie.

Still, a shiver runs up my spine when he keeps me under his spell, captivating me and making it hard for me to look away.

The spell is soon broken when the girl he's with steps in front of him, rubbing her boobs against his chest. I swallow past the pain and turn my attention back to Harlow, but not before I mistakenly see guilt ripple across his features.

I'm seeing things.

My feelings for him will never change, but I'm done making excuses for him. I'm done trying to tell myself that his actions mean nothing, that he doesn't mean to hurt me.

From now on, no other boy—especially Mason—is going to walk all over me.

My phone vibrates again, and I know it's my nan asking me where I am. I don't need to look. I have to say goodbye.

A lone tear slips free when I begin to trudge through the mud, making my way over to Harlow. I scan the area for Hannah and see her getting into a car with a woman wearing scrubs.

Harlow cuddles into Malik, soaking in his warmth and love. A part of me doesn't want to interrupt them, to sour their mood. They look so peaceful together.

Maybe I can just walk away quietly. They wouldn't even know I was gone.

Steeling my shoulders, I put on a brave façade and tap her on her shoulder. I need to say goodbye, to let her know she means everything to me.

Worry is etched across her face when she looks from Malik to me. She pulls me into her arms. "Are you okay?"

"No, I have to tell you something, and I want you to know that I didn't say anything before because I didn't know how to. Then last night, I decided to do the right thing."

I wait for Malik to leave. He's giving me the same look he gave me earlier, but instead of lingering and refusing to give us privacy, he gives me a chin lift.

"I'll be over there," he tells her, before kissing her. He then leaves, giving us the privacy I asked for.

As soon as he's out of earshot, I begin to sob. She pulls me into her arms, running a hand up and down my back. It only makes me cry harder, though no noise escapes me as I cling to her.

"What do you need to tell me?"

"He told me so many lies. He told me he'd wanted me for years, that he'd never met anyone like me before. I believed everything he ever said to me. Then that night, I gave myself to him. I gave him everything, and he doesn't even realise just how much he's taken from me." I angrily wipe away my tears.

"Hey, everything's going to be okay. What's wrong? Things will get better in time, Denny. You'll be crying over some other dickhead in a few months, I bet ya."

"That's the thing, Harlow. I don't have time," I admit, my shoulders shaking from the reality of it.

"What do you mean?" she asks, her fingers tensing on my arm.

"I'm leaving," I blurt out, stepping away. I have to do this quickly, like ripping a plaster off.

"What—like, going home?" she asks, but her expression falls. Deep down, she knows what I really mean. "We need to talk about this."

"No. My parents kicked me out. My nan has offered to let me live with her, so I'm moving to Wales."

"You can stay with us. Grams won't mind, and she has a spare room. Don't leave," she pleads, not understanding me.

"You don't understand, Harlow. It's not that simple. I *can't* stay here."

"Make me understand. We're friends and I'm here for you." She pauses, and I know she can see I've already made my decision. "What is it you're not telling me, Denny?"

"I'm pregnant."

My knees nearly buckle at saying it out loud. Harlow steadies me, pulling me in for a hug.

"Denny," she whispers.

I break, crying into her shoulder. "Now can you see why I can't be here?"

When she pulls back, she tries to mask her shock. Then her gaze goes to the side of us, to where Mason is watching us, and she narrows her eyes.

"Did he tell you to leave?"

"No," I whisper, trying to force the tears back. "He doesn't even know."

"Then we can fix this," she tells me, letting the tears pour down her cheeks.

I grab her arm, stopping her. "Would you want Malik to be with you because you were pregnant with his baby, or because he loved you?"

"But—"

"I can't do it, Harlow. I can't force him to be someone he isn't. I've tried to tell him, to talk to him, but each time, my heart broke a little more inside when I saw him with a different girl. I can't do this."

"Maybe—"

My phone vibrates again, so I squeeze her hand, giving her a grim smile. "I have to go."

"No, no," she calls out, pulling me back. Tears stream down her face now, and it hurts. I hate that I'm hurting her. "Just stay here. Let me go talk to him. We can sort this, I promise. Let me get Mason, okay?"

Knowing she isn't going to stop, I give her a nod, unable to find my voice. She walks off, and the second her back is turned, I run. I run to where my nan is waiting for me with the car running.

I'm just over the fence when I hear my name being called. "Denny! Stop!" Harlow cries.

"Wait, Denny. Don't do this," Mason yells, and I close my eyes as pain consumes me.

I jump in the car and turn to Nan. "Go. Please, go!" I croak out.

Nan glances out the window, struggling to decide what to do. I'm ready to scream when I see them getting closer.

"Please, Nan, go," I cry out.

She puts her foot down, squealing off the dirt path and onto the road.

I relax into the seat, leaning my head against the window as I look out into the darkness, thick tears streaming down my face.

Nan's hand rests over mine on my thigh, giving it a gentle squeeze. "Everything is going to be okay," she promises.

I don't bother correcting her.

I have nothing to say, because I know, deep in my soul, nothing is going to be okay. My heart is tearing apart inside of me, and with each mile we drive away, the worse it gets.

The only person who can make this better is the person we left chasing our taillights. And I'm never going to force him to be a dad, or make him be the guy I fell in love with.

It's over.

All of it is over.

CHAPTER
ONE

MASON - TWO AND A HALF MONTHS LATER

D ifferent day, same shit!

That seems to be the new motto in my life, ever since the day I found out Denny Smith is pregnant with my baby.

I spent months, if not more, trying to push the girl away; when all along I should have been winning her over. I thought I was doing what was best for her. I didn't deserve her, and I let the fear of my past define my future. It was something I said I'd never do, and I went and did it anyway.

And I hurt the girl who meant everything to me.

My change of heart isn't just about the baby either. It was mostly because of Denny. She was everything I wanted but didn't deserve. She was everything other girls weren't. And no one can replace or fill the void in my heart. When she left, I realised what I lost, and I have paid for it every day.

My dad cheated on my mother left, right and centre when we were kids. We saw the effect it had on her. And the abuse didn't end there. He constantly hit her, to the point she no longer had any fight left in her.

What if the apple didn't fall far from the tree? What if I turned out just like him and destroyed Denny? She was everything I wasn't, and I didn't want to take the risk of destroying her like my dad did my mother. No way. I cared for her way too much to even contemplate it.

Then the rules changed.

I found out she was pregnant five minutes after watching her drive out of my life. When Harlow said Denny was leaving town, I panicked and ran after her. The second the taillights disappeared in the distance, I turned to Harlow and asked why.

The words, "She's pregnant," still haunt me.

I did what I always do. I ran away from my problems, turned to the bottle, and pretended I didn't care. Our child would be better off without me.

But then I overheard Harlow telling Malik that Denny was coming home. She had been summoned by the courts to testify. I couldn't deny the feelings that revelation evoked inside of me. I wanted to see her. It was a slap to the face, and suddenly, I could no longer pretend I was okay with her living miles away. She belonged here. She belonged with me.

I tried to get Harlow to give me Denny's new number, even asked for her address so I could drive to her, but she wouldn't give up that information. I understood. I hurt her friend, and she was protecting her. So for two and a half months, I have been going stir crazy, scared I might never see her again.

She gets back into town tomorrow evening, and I've been working my arse off trying to get her surprise ready in time for her return.

It's one way to prove to her that I'm serious about us, about becoming a dad.

I wanted to get our own place, but once Maverick learned of my plans, he offered me the house we got permission to build in our garden. We even changed the layout upstairs, taking the four-bedroom house and turning it into a three with an en-suite.

It's finished and ready to be moved into, but I want to get the baby's room decorated first. It's on hold at the minute because I don't know if the baby is a boy or a girl. Plus, I'm guessing Denny will want to choose what goes in there.

I left it blank so that once I know everything Denny wants, I can deck it out and give her the best nursery she's ever imagined.

I scrub my hands down my face, groaning. Who am I kidding? Denny probably doesn't want to speak to me, let alone move in with me.

I can't let her raise our baby alone, miles away from me. This is karma coming back to bite me in the arse; something Harlow warned me about the day after I slept with Denny.

Fuck!

That night was one of the best nights of my life. I've fucked a lot of girls in my years, but never, and I mean *never*, have I ever felt connected to one like I did with Denny. We were both so caught up in the moment that it had taken me until the morning to realise she was a virgin. That's when everything went to shit. I flipped out, got scared, and ruined the best thing to ever happen to me.

When she told me she was a virgin, I looked into her big, dark emerald eyes and froze. All I could see was this vulnerable, perfect, young, beautiful woman in my bed, and I had already tainted her by taking her virginity. I didn't romance her, buy her flowers, or take her out on a date, and it made me realise just how alike my dad and I are. He would have most likely done the same thing. Instead of apologising and treating her the way she should have been treated by taking her out on a date, I pushed her away. I pushed and I pushed, to the point I think it may be too late for me to take it all back.

I made her believe I slept with all those women I threw in her face, when in truth, I could never keep my mind or eyes away from Denny long enough to fake it with another girl. I just wanted *her*, but I didn't want to ruin her life because of my own selfishness. She's perfect in every sense of the word, and she deserves more than I'll ever be able to give her.

The rules have changed though. We have a baby on the way. If that isn't proof enough that pushing her away was the worst thing I could ever have done, the ache I've had in my chest since the day she drove off would pretty much do it.

The day she left, I felt exactly the same way, if not worse, as the day she ran from me—the morning after I took her virginity. It was like my heart had been torn from my chest and I couldn't breathe. It hurt when she walked out of my room, tears streaming down her face, but it broke me more the day she got in that car and drove away.

I'll do anything to make sure she never looks at me the same way again.

A touch startles me from my thoughts, and I frown at the woman standing next to me.

"So?" she huffs, and I realise she must have been speaking to me while I drifted off into my own head.

Maverick ordered me to come into work, reminding me I'll need time off when Denny arrives, so I can make it up to her.

I agreed to take on the extra shifts, but only because I was under the impression work would keep me distracted. And it would have, had I not put a few extra staff on the rota tonight. I'm not needed, not when my deputy manager is on the floor too.

I kept messing up too, so I was only getting in the way of the others who were trying to work. Which is why I parked my arse on the stool at the end of the bar, and nursed a beer. I was finally beginning to relax, but then some woman walked over, trying to get my attention.

"Are you even listening to me?" she asks, and it's like a shrill echoing in my ear.

I wince, rubbing at my ears, before I turn to her. Her face, red and pinched, has me shuffling back a little. She looks like she's trying really hard not to scream at me right now.

I snort to myself. I've met hundreds of girls like her. She doesn't want to show her true colours just yet because she's still hoping she can seduce me into a quick fuck. And maybe a few months ago, she might have. Not now. Not now I know what I really want.

"I'm not," I deadpan, keeping my eyes locked on my beer.

My mind wanders back to Denny, and tomorrow. I wonder if

she'll show up; if she'll listen to me long enough to hear I'm really sorry. Or my biggest worry: if she has it in her to forgive me.

The chick next to me isn't put off by my remark. Instead, she becomes more desperate, and runs a hand down my arm.

"Maybe we could go somewhere quiet," she tells me, trying to sound seductive. In reality, she sounds like nails scratching down a chalkboard.

When she presses closer, rubbing her tits against my arm, I move my arm onto the bar, knocking her away from me.

My lips twist in disgust. "Look, love, I'm gay, and although you do have manly features, I prefer dick."

"Excuse me," she remarks, stepping back when I slide off the stool.

"Yes, excuse you," I snap, grabbing my jacket off the bar. I side-step her and head to the offices downstairs.

I need to do more than renovate a home to win Denny back. I have to work out a plan that everyone is on board with. Denny is more likely to listen if they are. My main priority is to get Harlow to agree. She's looking out for her friend, and I can understand that, but sometimes, that girl can be stubborn as shit. She reminds me of her nan in that aspect.

If it all works out, I could have Denny living with me by the end of the week—if not tomorrow. I'm not going to get myself too psyched up though.

I have a lot of ground to cover where Denny is concerned, and a lot to be forgiven for.

I'm no longer running from her though.

I'm running toward her.

And I will get her.

A Carter always gets what he wants.

CHAPTER
TWO

DENNY

rub a hand over my ever-growing baby bump. I'm only twenty-
one weeks gone, but my nan swears I look further along with
how large my bump is.

I can't wait to have another scan. I'm overdue one, but for three
weeks, I have been putting it off. Each time I think about it, I feel sick,
just like I did after I had the first one. It felt wrong to be there without
Mason. It's just one of the many times I've wondered if I made a
mistake in leaving.

"Are you sure you don't want me to stay with you?" Nan asks, still
the worrier.

"Nan, I'm fine. Honestly," I assure her.

"Are you sure? Have you spoken to Evan yet?"

My nan has driven me insane with her smothering. It comes from
a good place, and I love her for it, but sometimes it's too much.

As for my brother, he hasn't contacted me since I called him a
week ago to ask if I could crash at his place. It was the day after I
received my summons letter from the courts.

"Yes, Nan. Evan texted me earlier to let me know he's waiting for me outside the train station," I lie.

I don't want to worry her any more than she already is. She didn't like that I travelled alone from Wales to Coldenshire and has been calling me every five minutes since I boarded the train. I had downloaded a new romance novel to read, but I haven't even managed to get past the first page.

I would tell her about Harlow picking me up, but she warned me to stay away from her. She's anxious that Harlow's connection to the Carter's will bring him back into my life. She's worried how he'll react to seeing me and what it will do to my mental health again. Her concerns are justifiable, since I spent the first few weeks in my new home crying and sleeping. It hurt to leave, and I had a lot I needed to come to terms with. Becoming a single mother being one of them. Another because I knew how much Mason would hate me for keeping the pregnancy from him.

"Thank goodness, Denny. That boy really needs to answer that mobile phone of his. Call me when you arrive, and if Evan isn't there to pick you up—"

"He will be; so stop worrying," I plead, interrupting. Picking up the newspaper some guy left on his seat a few stops back, I begin to fan myself. The mid-August heat is overbearing. I can't wait to get off this hot, stuffy train. My silent prayers are answered when the intercom announces the next stop. "Nan, the next stop is mine. I need to gather my stuff so I don't get trampled on while trying to get it all together."

"Of course. You go on now. Don't forget to call me. And make sure you drink plenty of water. And remember to take those vitamins. I packed a spare packet in your suitcase."

Rolling my eyes, I answer. "Thank you. Now stop worrying. Speak to you later."

"Okay. I will," she tells me, letting out a sigh. "Love you, my sweet girl."

"Love you too," I tell her, before ending the call.

I shove my phone back into my handbag and quickly grab my

hand luggage and suitcase. Once it's all together, I make my way towards the door and place them on the floor.

Forgetting I didn't message Harlow, I quickly pull my phone back out of my bag and type one out.

DENNY: Are you still okay to pick me up? I'm nearly there.

When she doesn't answer right away, I begin to worry. Just as I'm about to put my phone back into my bag, it vibrates with a message.

HARLOW: I'm in the car park waiting. X

A smile spreads across my face and excitement bubbles inside of me. I can't wait to see her. We've spoken occasionally over the phone, but for the first few weeks, I couldn't speak to anyone. When we would chat, she kept talking about *him*—or trying to—and I couldn't listen to it. It wasn't until she promised not to bring him up that I started to talk to her more.

It hurt too much to think about him. Even now, knowing we'll be in the same town, my stomach turns with unease. And something else.

The light next to the door flashes and I grab my bags, preparing myself for the doors to open. As soon as they do, I delight in the cool breeze for a moment, forgetting I need to get off. People begin to shuffle past me in a hurry to get off the train, some knocking into me.

I growl low in my throat, livid at how rude people can be.

"*Hello*? Pregnant woman here, and carrying two bags, assholes," I snap when another businessman knocks past me.

I'm about to step off the train and onto the platform, when my bags are suddenly pulled from my arms. Before I can sumo wrestle the asshole who has taken them from me, I'm struck still.

It's *him*.

Before I can process what's happening, he's stepping closer, his calloused hands gripping me under my armpits and lifting me off the train.

He slowly sets me down onto the platform and stares down at me. I don't know what to do, or what to say. I'm in two minds. Should I scream and slap him, or should I be the bigger person and thank him, then leave?

"Hello, Denny," he greets, his voice deep and raspy.

Much to my disappointment, I have the same reaction to him as I always do. My skin is covered in goose bumps, a shiver races down my spine, and my stomach flutters.

I hate that he still has a powerful effect on me. He put me through so much. I don't get it. It's like I'm a glutton for punishment or something.

I clear my throat, trying to steel my nerves. "Hello, Mason."

We gaze into each other's eyes for what seems like hours. I kind of prepared myself for this moment, and I'm glad I put on my white sun dress that swirls around my knees. If I was going to see him again after all this time, I was going to look good for it. I just didn't expect it to be today. I'm grateful I didn't wear my joggers today, which was a strong possibility since I don't have many clothing choices recently due to my size.

He's changed, even if my reaction to him hasn't. His hair is longer, his eyes have dark circles around them, and he hasn't shaved for a while. His chocolate brown eyes are no longer sparkling. They seem dull, full of sadness, pain, and regret.

My heart clenches at the sight of him. All this time I assumed he'd be grateful I left. It was what he wanted: me out of his life. But the person in front of me... he looks like a man with regrets.

This is too much. It all is. Tears gather in my eyes, and I look around for an exit. I know I can't run, but I can't stay either.

I grab the handle of my case and pick my bag up off the floor. I give him one last look, before I leave him there, standing on a nearly empty platform.

"Why didn't you tell me?" he blurts out, sounding somewhere between angry and sad about it.

I stop and close my eyes. The reminder of why I didn't tell him is painful. He touches my arm, but as quick as his hand is there, it's gone.

I turn to face him, contemplating what to do.

Does he deserve an answer?

He's occupied my thoughts for so long, I should know what to say, or what to do. But the truth of the matter is... I have no clue.

"I never had the chance," I whisper, my gut clenching.

I knew Harlow would tell him about the baby, and I don't begrudge her for it. She never told me outright that she'd informed him, but it's Harlow. She needs to fix things. And it wasn't like I told her to keep it a secret. I never wanted it to be a secret. I just never got the opening to tell him.

I'm mad at myself more than anything. If I had just stopped and turned around the night I left, we wouldn't be having this conversation right now. It would have already been had.

As important as this conversation is, I'm hot, hungry, and extremely tired. I'm surprised I didn't fall asleep with my nan yapping away on the phone.

I'm also not ready for this conversation. Not yet. I had hoped to avoid seeing him for a little longer.

"You didn't? Because if I'm remembering correctly, you had time the night you left. I was right there. But you told Harlow. You could have told me any time, or even one of my brothers, but you didn't. Did it even occur to you that I would want to know? That I deserved to know; to be there for you and the baby?"

My head snaps up, my blood pressure rising. I'd like to blame it on the pregnancy hormones, but no, this is all me.

How dare he push all the blame onto me.

"I'm sorry," I reply bitterly. "I guess I should have texted you. Oh, no, wait—you blocked me. Or maybe I should have told you every time I saw you? Oh, that's right, you ran like a little boy and avoided me." I place my index finger on my lip. "Better yet, maybe I should have told you when you were with one of your hook-ups? Wait…" I bite out, tapping my temple. "My heart was too busy breaking, because, you know, I have one."

"Denny," he starts, but I hold my hand up.

"Mason, I tried to fucking tell you over and over again. *You* were the one always too fucking busy avoiding *me*. I'm the one who had to go through this on my own. I'm a fucking teenager, for fuck's sake, and I had to do it on my own. And when I finally did find the courage to tell someone, my parents told me what a disgrace I was, and that if I wanted to keep living under their roof, I needed to have an abortion. You weren't there, Mason. So don't you dare place any of this on me."

He's watching me, lips parted, guilt etched into his features. "Denny, I—"

I ignore him and instead continue, my voice steadily rising. "If you had given me the time of day, I would have told you, Mason. I would have."

I hiccup, wiping at the angry tears falling down my cheeks. I'm beginning to gather attention from the other passengers around us.

He reaches for me, but then pulls back before he can touch me.

"Denny, I'm so fucking sorry. For everything. What I did after I slept with you, I just... I—" He stops suddenly, his shoulders deflating. When he looks up, all I see is sorrow. "Come on. The others are waiting to see you."

He grabs the handle of my case and lifts the other over his shoulder, then heads for the exit. I follow behind at a slower pace, my mind reeling over what was said. I've been trying so hard to move on from him that I didn't expect my old feelings to resurface. Yet I can't deny that they are there. I want to slap myself for feeling this way. He hurt me, and I have to remember that.

"Welcome home," is yelled when I exit through the door leading out into the carpark. I take a step back, going solid when I see all the Carter's and their granddad standing there; Harlow and her grams with them. I'm rooted to the spot, a lump forming in my throat.

I didn't think anyone would want to speak to me again after I upped and left the way I did. I certainly didn't expect this reception, not after I left without telling Mason I was pregnant.

"What are you guys doing here?" I ask, coming unglued.

Harlow is the first to step away from the group. She comes rushing towards me, only slowing down once she's close so she doesn't knock me to the ground. She pulls me in for a hug, and I wrap my arms around her, having missed her like crazy.

"I've missed you," she cries into my shoulder, before pulling back and scanning me up and down. "Bloody hell, you look stunning, Denny. I can't believe how big your belly is."

I run a hand over my stomach, feeling a little self-conscious.

"Yeah, babe, what are you packing under that dress? Can I see?" Max flirts, coming up to give me a hug.

Laughing, I hug him back, quickly pulling away when I hear a growl close by. Max's gaze drifts down towards my cleavage—which is pretty impressive right now. I guess it's a perk that comes with being pregnant. I snort, slapping his shoulder when he doesn't look away.

"Move your eyes, dickhead," Mason grits out, making me jump.

I didn't even realise he was so close. Now that I'm fully aware, I can feel the heat coming off of him.

Max winces, shrugging apologetically. "Sorry."

He doesn't sound sorry, only sorry he has to look away. He's shoved out of the way by his twin brother—Myles—who sweeps me in for a hug.

"It's good to have you back. The gang has been lost without you," he mutters, before stepping back.

"Thanks," I whisper, feeling overwhelmed. I hid my pregnancy from all of them, yet they're all here welcoming me back with open arms. Literally.

Malik gives me a chin lift, which makes me smile. It seems some things didn't change around here.

Harlow leans against him, looking up at him with a goofy smile. Seeing them so loved up and happy, it makes my heart swell.

"Welcome home, sweetie," Harlow's grams—Joan—greets, before giving me a hug.

"Thank you."

Mark—Mason's Granddad—does the same before moving back to Joan's side. Harlow mentioned over the phone that the two had gotten together and are officially living together now. But seeing them together like this... it's cute.

Maverick—the eldest of the Carter siblings—greets me last. His eyes are warm and soft when he approaches me. We haven't really spoken to each other in the past, so it's surprising to see him here with everyone else.

"Welcome to the family, darlin'."

His words shock me, but when he brings me in for a hug, it completely baffles me.

"Thank you," I whisper back once I've found my voice.

"We've cleaned out Malik's old room over at Mark's for you to stay in, sweetie. Don't worry, it's only until the boys finish off the painting in the new house, then you can stay there," Joan explains, taking me off guard.

What house? What paint? I look at Mason for answers, but he's staring at me like he's trying to gauge my reaction.

"I'm sorry? I'm confused," I admit, wanting someone to explain.

"Well, you can't live in a house full of boys with a new baby on the way, silly girl. With Mark and Malik living with us now, there is only Max, Maverick and Myles living there. Still, you, Mason, and the baby will need your own space."

My head whips to Mason in shock. I'm getting whiplash with all this new information. Harlow never mentioned this on the phone.

I narrow my gaze on Mason whilst still trying to process everything. This is not how I saw my welcome home.

It makes me wonder what, exactly, he told them. Because moving in with him? That can't be right. He broke my heart without even blinking.

And did they all really think I could live with someone who has a long line of women visiting his bedroom every night?

I clench my teeth, trying to control my anger as I address them. "I'm sorry, but I think you've all got your wires crossed. I'm not staying long, and definitely not with Mason. I'm going to crash at my brother's house until the court case is over, and then I'll be going back home to live with my nan."

Everyone goes quiet and sneaks glances at Mason, like they're waiting for him to contradict me or something. I do the same, wondering what the hell I'm missing, only to find him glaring down at me.

"Like fuck you are, Denny," he snaps.

I place my fists on my hips. "Excuse me?" I bark.

"Why? What did you do?" he replies sarcastically.

"What the hell is your problem, Mason?"

"*You are.* You're not moving back to your nan's, Denny. We're having a baby together, for Christ's sake."

"News flash, Mason: *I'm* having a baby. Not you. You didn't want anything to do with me before you found out. Now all of a sudden you expect me to come running back to you, to obey your demands? Yeah, I don't bloody think so."

"Yes, actually, I do. Maybe if you had told me in the first place, we wouldn't be in this mess."

"Are you telling me I should have had an abortion?" I yell, feeling my stomach turn. This was one of my biggest fears when I realised I would need to tell him. "Get lost, you prick. I'm not asking you to be a part of this baby's life, or to be with me. I wouldn't want to tie you down, or, God forbid, make you do something you don't want to do."

With that, I grab my suitcase and carry on towards the taxi rank, ignoring his and everyone else's shocked faces. Tears are streaming down my face, and my heart is pumping so hard I worry about passing out. I can't believe he said that.

I rub my chest with my free hand, trying to get rid of the dull ache. When I see a free taxi, I sag with relief, but it's short-lived when I hear boots crunching into gravel behind me.

"Wait," Mason calls out, his tone urgent.

I pause and close my eyes briefly. I don't want another argument, and I don't want to cause another scene in front of loads of people.

He walks around me to block me from leaving, his expression filled with guilt and pain. "I'm sorry. I keep messing this up. I just don't know how to make this up to you. I should have asked you about the living arrangements first. I know we have a lot to sort through when it comes to us, but, Denny, I want to be with you. I want us to be a family."

My pulse begins to race. For the first time, he has said everything I dreamed he would say, but at what cost? Is it because I'm carrying his child?

"Why now? Because of the baby?" I croak out, and for the first time, I'm jealous of my baby.

It's childish and uncalled for, but I can't help it. The love of my life finally wants me, and it isn't even because of me. The urge to laugh hits me, and not because I find this funny. But because the irony isn't lost on me.

I'm not one of those girls who settles; not anymore. Maybe a few months ago I wouldn't have cared why he wanted to be with me. Now? There's more than just me to think about.

"What? *No.* That isn't why." He pauses to run a hand over his face. "Yes, it's one of the reasons, but it's not the only one. I wanted to be with you before you even knew you wanted to be with me, Denny. Look, we have loads to talk about, and I have some explaining to do, but can we do it tomorrow, after you've had a chance to sleep on everything that's been said today? I want to get you home. It's late, and I bet you're hungry."

It's like my stomach can understand his words, because it chooses that moment to rumble, loud enough for Mason to hear. He sends me a knowing smirk, and I roll my eyes.

I can't trust his intentions. A lot doesn't add up. He's either playing me again or he genuinely means what he said. Either way, now isn't the time to process it. I'm hungry, and I'm dying to take a nap.

I sigh, my shoulders dropping. "Yes to food, but no to staying with you guys. I promised my brother I'd be there to look after his house," I lie, not really knowing whether my brother will be there or not. He never said.

"Well, don't get used to being there, Denny. One way or another, you'll be coming to live with me. I'm not letting you go this time."

I roll my eyes again, not believing his idle threat, and move to pick up my bags, but Mason swoops in and grabs them from me.

I guess he learned some manners whilst I was gone too.

———

I 'm completely shattered by the time Mason pulls onto my brother's street. We all ended up going for a meal together, and I think I ate more than the brothers, which is saying something.

Maverick and the twins were the first to bail. Maverick had to get to work, and Max and Myles went to meet some girls from school. Harlow and Malik left not long after to go watch a movie at the cinema. I did ask Mark to drop me back when he went to leave with Joan, but Mason stopped him with a warning glare, saying he'd be taking me.

Being this close to him, it's bringing back memories. Painful ones.

"There aren't any lights on," Mason comments as he pulls up outside my brother's bungalow. He looks over at the deserted house. "Are you sure you don't want to stay at ours?"

I've tried calling Evan a few times since I arrived in town, but they all went straight to voicemail. I'm starting to worry I'll have to take Mason up on his offer and actually go stay with them. I don't want to do that.

When I see my brother, I'm going to kill him. He knew I was coming today.

All I want to do is curl up in a nice snuggly bed. I don't want to think about Mason or the things he said. And I have an inkling that if I leave with him tonight, he'll talk to me until I give in. I'm not ready for that.

I'm still reeling over the fact he hasn't demanded I have an abortion—although that's no longer an option. Not that it ever was. But this… I never considered this greeting.

Which is why I need him to leave.

I need to think, and I can't to do that with him around, jumbling my mind.

"Yeah, I'm sure. Maybe he fell asleep waiting for me. I did tell him I'd be here over two hours ago." I don't like lying to him, but it's necessary in this moment. If I tell him I have no clue where Evan is, he won't let me leave the car until we're at his.

"I'll get your bags while you go and knock on the door," he offers, sounding sceptical. He scans the area when he slides out, and I follow, pulling my cardigan around my waist. It isn't the best neighbourhood to live in, but it does have a low crime rate. That could be because the people living here probably don't have anything worth robbing.

I walk up the path to the door and rap my knuckles a few times, before noticing the doorbell on the side. I push the button, tapping my foot restlessly when I hear Mason heading up the path behind me.

Sweat begins to trickle down my neck, and it isn't because it's a muggy night. It's because I know Mason is about to get his way.

"I don't think he's here, Tink."

Gah, that freaking nickname! I hate it yet completely love it at the same time. I look nothing like her now—not that I did before. Though with my white-blond hair, short height, and button nose, I can see why he would see the resemblance between me and the Disney fairy.

"Hey," a beautiful brunette calls as she jogs across the garden. She comes to a stop in front of us, panting a little. I can't help but take in her short shorts, and her tiny spaghetti strap top that shows a large amount of skin. I feel like crying at the sight of her. She is beautiful.

Old habits have me looking up at Mason to see if he's checking her out. I'm surprised to find he isn't, and that his gaze is on me. His chocolate brown eyes bore into mine, and I try not to fall under their spell.

"Um, hey," the woman greets again, waving her hand.

I force a smile. "Sorry. What was you saying?"

She beams, relaxing slightly. "I'm Lexi, Evan's next-door neighbour. He told me…"

I stop listening when Mason steps closer, his arm brushing against mine. I inhale, trying to compose myself when he smirks.

"You are Denny, right?" Lexi asks, and I focus my attention on her.

My cheeks heat when I realise I've been gawking at Mason. "I'm sorry. Yes, I'm Denny, but I missed what you said."

She laughs, waving me off. "It's fine. I guess if my bloke was as hot as him, I'd be pretty out of it too."

"He's not my—"

"You don't need to explain," she tells me. "I'm friends with your brother, and I live right next door. He came by yesterday to let me know he was heading out of town on a job. He asked if I could give you the key when you arrived. I've been waiting for you to get here for hours. I had started to think you weren't coming, or I had missed you, until I heard a car pull up."

"I'm sorry for keeping you waiting. And thank you." I take the keys, giving her a smile in return.

"Great. I've done your room and cleaned it up a bit. I knew Evan wouldn't have touched the place, and I was right. The only room I refuse to tackle is his bedroom," she explains, scrunching her nose up.

A giggle escapes me because I can only imagine. When Evan still lived at home, it was a nightmare. He never picked up his dirty laundry at all and always had food shoved under his bed. It was gross. If he still lives like that then I feel deeply sorry for the woman standing in front of me.

"That bad, huh?"

"Something like that," she admits, chuckling. "He didn't know what you'd need, so I went in last night to see what was there before he left. When I asked where you'd be sleeping, he thought you'd just stay in his bed, since he didn't have any sheets for the spare." Her lips pull out as she rolls her eyes. "Luckily, he listened to reason and left some money with me to get everything you need. It's all in there, and the change is on the kitchen counter."

"That sounds like him. Thank you for doing that and for going to so much trouble. You didn't need to."

"Trust me, I did," she warns me. "I'll leave you to get settled in, but if you need anything, please let me know. I only live next door." She groans, shaking her head. "I said that already, didn't I?"

I rub my hand over my rounded belly, my laugh turning into a yawn.

Mason steps closer, brushing his hand over my arm. "I think that means you're ready for bed."

Lexi nods, before giving us a wave. "Speak to you soon."

"Bye," I call out, before turning back to Mason. I'm ready to say goodnight and thank him for dropping me off, when he steps closer, looking on edge.

"I don't think you should stay here by yourself. It doesn't feel right you being alone. You need people around you," he tells me. "And this part of town isn't the best."

"We've talked about this already," I remind him, exhaling heavily. "I'm not ready. You spent months pushing me away, and then all of a sudden, I'm back and you want me to move in." I throw my hands up before letting them drop. "It's all too soon. I need space."

He runs a hand through his hair. "I didn't want to push you away. I thought I was—" He stops and takes a deep breath. "We can talk about this when we have more time. Let me stay the night, at least until your brother gets back, so you aren't alone."

"I'm a big girl, Mase. I've had my nan spoiling me rotten back home. She hasn't given me a moment's peace. I'll enjoy the space."

"That's not your home," he growls, his shoulders tensing.

"Huh?"

"*Here* is your home. Well, not here, here—here with me."

"Please, Mase, I'm tired. Can we do this tomorrow?"

Another yawn leaves my mouth, making him chuckle. I smile tiredly up at him, before locating the right key to the door.

"Can I at least see you tomorrow?" he asks as he places my luggage inside the door.

Unsure what I should do, it takes me a moment to agree. "Just don't expect too much from me."

"There's something I need to know before I leave." He swallows, gripping the doorframe. "Are we having a boy or a girl? And is everything okay?"

Emotion clogs my throat. "It's fifty-fifty at the moment."

"What do you mean?" he asks, scratching the back of his neck. His biceps bulge against his white T-shirt, and I inwardly sigh. I know first-hand how they feel wrapped around me.

"I have an appointment at the hospital on Friday. They were happy to transfer me. I missed the last two because it didn't feel right going without you. It was hard without anyone really." I shrug, trying to hide how much it hurt me. But it's useless. My expression falls, revealing how much it bothered me.

"Oh. Can, um… can I come with you?" he asks, hope in his tone as he gazes briefly at my rounded stomach.

"I'd really like that," I reply earnestly around a ball of emotion in my throat.

He grins big, and there's a bounce in his step as he steps back. "Okay. Good. Yeah." He grins big as he takes a step outside.

I follow, standing in the open doorway as he leaves. He turns around to face me, his eyes shinier than they were earlier. My stomach flips at the intensity of this moment. He's watching me like I handed him the world—or a day pass at the Playboy mansion.

I wave, giving him a small smile. "See you tomorrow."

"See you tomorrow, beautiful," he calls back, winking.

Something from the corner of my eye catches my attention as Mason gets in the car. Chills run down my back, and the hairs on the back of my neck stand on end, when I see a shadowy figure standing across the road.

I jump when Mason pulls away, then revert my attention to the willowy figure.

It's gone.

Quickly stepping inside, I bolt the door shut, cursing my pregnancy paranoia.

It was only the other day that I was paranoid an old woman was trying to steal my hamburger.

Just to be safe, I walk around the rest of the house, double checking everything's locked.

By the time I'm finished, I'm completely exhausted. My legs and back ache so badly I can't think of doing anything but going to sleep.

I head into the room Lexi kindly sorted out for me and lie down on the bed. The second my head hits the pillow, I succumb to the darkness.

Everything else can wait.

CHAPTER
THREE

DENNY

Morning light streams through the window, the warmth hitting my face. I groan, and roll to my other side to block it out. Even if I wasn't so tired, I don't have the energy to get up and shut the curtains.

I just need sleep.

And as I finally get comfortable, and in the stage of not being awake, or fully asleep, there's loud banging on the door. I scream into the pillow, muffling the sound.

I only need a few hours of sleep. Just a few hours.

The one thing I dislike about being pregnant is not being able to lie down on my stomach. I'm so used to sleeping that way, with my legs and arms spread, but my bump makes it impossible. It feels unnatural not being able to do it. And uncomfortable.

It's also a great position when you want to block out unwanted noises—like someone knocking on your door at God knows what time in the morning.

Sliding my legs off the side of the bed, I pull myself up into a sitting position. I silently curse when I take in the crinkled dress I didn't change out of last night.

Using the bedside table as support, I lift myself up off the bed. I catch sight of my reflection in the mirror hanging on the wall, and cringe. I run a hand over my wild blonde hair, which has lightened in the sun, and try to tame it as much as I can, to no avail.

The knocking gets louder, and more persistent. I growl low in my throat as I head out of the room. Still half asleep and in a new place, I misplace the sofa and stub my toe on the corner.

"Argh, fuck! Ow!" I cry out, really wanting to jump up and down in pain, but my large stomach prevents me from doing anything. Instead, I have to grit my teeth and breathe in and out until the pain subsides.

The banging continues, and I narrow my gaze on the door.

"Alright! Alright!" I yell, deciding I'm going to kill whoever is on the other side.

Pulling the door open, I'm surprised to find it's Harlow. She gives me a sheepish smile as she fiddles with the hem of her top. "Hey."

When her bottom lip begins to tremble, I open the door further, scanning for Malik. Since the attack, he hasn't left her side, so I'm surprised when I find her alone.

"Hey, what's wrong?"

She links her fingers together, unable to meet my gaze. "Can we talk?"

"Sure, come in. I'm sorry it took me a while to answer. I've only just got up."

"I'm sorry. Did I wake you?" she asks, pausing in her appraisal of the room.

"Nah," I lie. "Would you like a cup of tea?"

"Sure."

Heading into the kitchen, I quickly pop the kettle on whilst also putting some bread in the toaster. I turn to Harlow while the electronics get to work. "C'mon, tell me—what's on your mind?"

"Am I that easy to read?" she muses.

I nod, grabbing the butter out of the fridge when the toast pops up. I reply as I spread it. "Yes, so spill."

"I didn't want to worry you when you had so much going on, which is why I've not mentioned it until now," she begins, fiddling with the salt and pepper shaker. "But Grams started to look into why they were taking so long with the court case. She was worried they were stringing it along for reasons we weren't privy to."

"What did she find?" I ask, dropping the knife to the counter.

"Not much, but then today, the police finally released the information as to why. It's because the case is still in an ongoing investigation."

"What do you mean, it's ongoing?" I ask her, swallowing the toast with difficulty. I don't have a good feeling about this, and going by the look on Harlow's face, neither does she.

The case was straight forward. Davis drugged her, kidnapped her, and was going to rape her. He shouldn't just be prosecuted for those crimes, but also for leaving the mental scars Harlow will always carry.

"Can you remember the day you left?"

I look away. I will never forget the day I left. I thought I'd never breathe again when Nan and I drove away. "Yeah."

"Hannah left that night and got into a car…"

"Yeah, with some woman wearing scrubs," I finish, wondering where this is going. I barely remember that night, but I do remember that.

I don't know why Harlow is mentioning her. I hate the bitch for what she originally planned to do to Harlow. I should have beaten her arse when I had the chance.

I've known Hannah a long time. She was always the school bitch, but what she was going to do to Harlow went far beyond anything she had done before. She needs to be held accountable for it all.

"That's it. I couldn't remember…" she murmurs, trailing off.

Her face pales as she bites her bottom lip, looking torn. There's something else—something she isn't telling me—which isn't like her. She tells me pretty much everything.

"Harlow, please just tell me what is wrong. You're starting to worry me now."

When she looks up, her gaze is frantic. "She disappeared that night."

"Um, what do you mean disappeared?"

"Her mum said she dropped her off at home before she left for work, and hasn't seen her since. At first, her mum thought she went to stay with her dad in London. She's been known to do that during the holidays, but he hasn't heard from her in a while either. Now they're worried."

I step forward, rubbing her arm when I can see she's genuinely upset over it. "She's probably hiding because she's ashamed of what she did. She's going to get in trouble, and she knows it."

"That's what I thought too, but then... Oh God," she murmurs, taking in a breath.

"Hey, it will be okay. They'll find her."

"You don't get it. When the solicitor called this morning, he told us the trial keeps getting postponed because she's one of the main witnesses to the case and they need her. And now they've found the jacket she was wearing the last time she was seen, and it was covered in blood. They've linked it to the case," she explains.

Well shit!

"How do they reckon it's linked to this case? She pissed off a lot of people and bullied loads more. Plus, Davis is in custody until the hearing, so it's not like he can do anything to her. You shouldn't be worrying about this."

"I know. I know I shouldn't, but I can't help it. What if he's got someone to hurt her like he was going to hurt me? Denny, I don't think I could live with myself. I feel like this is all my fault," she cries, and that's when I realise why it's eating it at her.

Harlow has a heart of gold. She's pure. She is the only person I know who could feel this way towards someone who made her life hell and had a hand in nearly having her raped.

If I were in her shoes, I'd be happy she was gone. I don't wish her harm in the way Harlow was nearly hurt, but the girl has ruined too many lives.

"Harlow, do not feel bad for that bitch. If something bad has happened to Hannah, then that isn't on you. It's on her for getting mixed up with Davis in the first place. Both of them need to take responsibility for their actions. They only have themselves to blame, hon. Don't take that unnecessary guilt on." I take in a deep breath and hand her a cup of tea. "Let's go sit down."

She nods, taking the mug from me, and follows me into the living room, taking a seat on the sofa. I sit on the other end and curl my feet up, then rest the mug on my stomach.

She chews on her thumbnail, leaning back against the sofa.

"I feel so bad. I can't help it," she sniffs. "Her mum came by to see us not long after the solicitor called. She was so torn up over it all. She wanted to visit sooner, to ask if we knew anything, but she was told to keep it under wraps. They didn't want to scare off the person who may be involved with her disappearance."

"Oh God, what did she say?" I ask, feeling bad for her mum.

"She kept apologising for Hannah's behaviour. Then begged us to tell her where she was and what had happened to her. Once she realised we had no idea, she began to calm down. But still… it was awful," she admits. "She kept saying it was all her fault, that she didn't protect her emotionally when her and Hannah's dad got divorced. Hannah got caught up in the middle and it changed her. She feels guilty for not paying closer attention."

My stomach sinks, and I can't help but reach for it, gently brushing the palm of my hand over my bump. I never want my little bean to go through that. I've personally never been through it, but I can imagine it must be hard for a child stuck in the middle of a messy divorce.

"It still doesn't excuse Hannah for what she did."

"I know," Harlow agrees, breaking eye contact. "Do you think I'm a bad person for worrying about what will happen in court now she's not here to testify?" She looks up, her eyes flooded with tears. "Do you think he will walk free?"

I try to shuffle closer, but my big belly keeps me glued to the sofa. Instead, I reach out, taking her hand. "No, I don't think you're a bad person for worrying about that. I'd be the same. But they have a solid case, Harlow."

"I'm just so scared," she blubbers, shoving her face into her hands.

I can't bear to see her so broken anymore. Gripping the arm of the chair, I try to heave myself up from the sofa, only to fall back down. I groan, shuffling to the edge a little.

I fall back, becoming sweaty and tired already.

Why did my brother have to buy such a deep sofa?

"Do you need some help?" Harlow asks, smothering a giggle.

I groan, turning to face her. "I'm supposed to be the one helping you out here, not the other way around."

She gets up from the sofa and comes to stand in front of me, then takes my hand and helps me up. "It's the thought that counts," she tells me, her smile not reaching her eyes.

Once I'm up, I pull her in for a hug, which becomes awkward with my stomach in the way. Sighing, I pull back. "Everything is going to be okay. You'll see. She'll turn up in no time and everything will be okay."

She's wiping under her eyes, when there's a knock on the door. I turn in that direction, my eyebrows pulling together. "Did someone put an ad in the local paper about my arrival or something?"

She laughs, shaking her head. "That should be Malik and Mason with food," she explains. "They reluctantly let me come in first so I could have some girl time."

"Mason's here? With Malik? And food?" I squeak, looking down at my wrinkled clothes in horror.

Harlow scans my outfit, her lips twitching. "Well, it's midday in all fairness. We thought you'd be up already."

"Crap! I'm just going to have a quick shower and change my clothes," I rush out, walking out of the room at a fast clip.

I ignore Harlow's laughter and comment over me waddling out of the room. I don't care. The last time I tried to run, I pissed myself.

———

alf an hour later, I'm walking back into the front room, wearing another sundress. This was the first and only maternity item I was willing to buy. The coral sundress crosses over at the cleavage and the elastic band sits under my bust, which is comfortable around my bump. It's a style that will fit as I continue to grow. It's one of my favourite things to wear, and if I could wear this every day, I would.

"Fuck!"

My gaze collides with Mason's when I hear his voice. His gaze runs over my body, and I brush my hand down my dress self-consciously.

I can see the appreciation in his eyes and the desire he does nothing to hide. It doesn't make me feel any better about how I look. I've gained weight, and not just around my bump. My boobs and arse are much bigger too.

Finding my voice, I say, "Hey."

His gaze snaps up. "We, um, we got you a burger and stuff. I didn't know what you wanted, so I got you a bit of everything," he explains, pointing to the bag on the coffee table. "The woman at the counter said you're not allowed to eat raw eggs whilst pregnant, as well as bunch of other stuff, and I already knew you couldn't drink coffee. I guess there's a list somewhere of what you can and can't eat. I'll find it and make a copy." He rubs the back of his neck, glancing down at the bag like he's unsure.

I melt every time he questions himself, because it means he cares and wants to get it right.

Taking a step further into the room, I reply. "No need. My nan made one. I'll email it to you," I admit, shrugging. "Raw fish is another too, amongst other stuff. I'm just glad I'm not craving any of them."

He looks up from getting a burger out of the bag, and pauses. "What do you mean?"

"Well, my nan told me once that her friend had a craving for sucking bath water out of a sponge. Do not ask me how she got that craving. I went over it in my head because to crave something, aren't you meant to have tasted it before? Then I wondered what she was doing with a sponge in her mouth, and it kept going from there," I ramble. "I tried to ask Nan, but she wouldn't answer. I'm just glad I don't have any."

His eyes widen. "A sponge? Really?" he asks disbelievingly.

Harlow grabs her drink off the coffee table. "She's right. My mum once told me she had a craving for my dad's aftershave. She said she hated it whenever he wasn't around for her to sniff it," Harlow adds, giving me a wink.

"Why didn't she just buy his aftershave?" Malik asks, taking a bite from his burger.

Even though I've not long had some toast, my mouth waters from the smell, so I pick up the bag Mason pointed to earlier and grab a burger before taking a seat in the armchair.

"She said it wasn't the same. They tried spraying it on a T-shirt for her to wear, the craving was that bad, but when he left for work, she broke down crying and begged him to come home. I guess it wasn't just the aftershave, but my dad's scent too," she explains, sighing wistfully. "It's romantic when you think about it. I loved it when they told me stories like that."

When she gets lost in thought, I know she's thinking of them.

Malik, seeing her distress, grabs her around the waist and lifts her into his lap. She squirms and tries to get off, but then ends up in giggles when he gives her a stern look.

I'm envious of the pair being so in love with each other.

Sensing I'm being watched, I glance to the side, finding Mason watching me with a curious expression. I open my mouth—to say what, I don't know.

Malik interrupts before I can form a word. "We thought we'd all go out for the day," he offers. "We need to meet Maverick and Max at the club first, if that's okay with you?"

"The club?" I question, my jaw dropping. It's the one place Mason and Malik would never take me or Harlow before. At first, it didn't bother me that he kept me separate from that part of his life, but as time went on, I became paranoid. It felt like he was hiding something. "I thought we weren't allowed in there?"

"You're eighteen, angel. You can go in there whenever you like now. But you won't."

I glare at Mason. "Says who? You just said I'm eighteen and can go where I like." I arch an eyebrow, daring him to continue. How dare he tell me where I can and can't go!

"It gets packed in there on nights and weekends. There is no way I'm going to risk you getting bumped into by someone. Fuck that! You and the baby could be hurt."

I feel myself soften at his concern. He also has a point. One knock could do the world of damage, and my baby's life is something I'd rather not gamble with.

"Okay, so what are we going to do?" I ask, ignoring Malik whispering what must be dirty words to Harlow, if her red face and giggles are anything to go by.

"It's a surprise. But we should get going," Mason explains, smiling.

I smile shyly back. I love this side of Mason. It's the side I had of him before we slept together.

A phone begins to ring and Harlow leans up, grabbing her phone out of her pocket.

"It's Max," she reveals, before answering. "Hey Max. Yes. Why? We're on our way. We had to stop off and get food." She pauses, letting out a groan. "Oh my god, stop. We'll buy you something when we get there, for God's sake. All right. See you in a bit." She ends the call before looking over at me. "Max is getting impatient, so grab your stuff before he comes here himself."

Laughing, I get back up from the chair. "I'll just grab my phone and bag from my bedroom, and then I'll be ready," I tell her, before rushing down the hall to my room.

———

After picking up Max and Maverick, we drive for thirty minutes before coming to a stop outside one of the biggest parks in our area. It's beautiful here, and today, it's rammed with people.

The minute we exit the car, I hear music blaring all around us and kids screaming on rides. With everything going on in my life, I forgot about the carnival. I normally head into town to watch the floats drive through, then follow behind to the park where all the real fun begins. My favourite had always been to head over to where the band plays in the centre of the park. I could sit or stand, bopping my head to the music for most of the day.

We're at the back of where that goes on. We're closer to all of the amusements and rides.

I bounce on my toes when I spot the candyfloss stand.

I press my hands together. "Can we get some candyfloss, please?" I squeal, delighted.

"Why don't you find somewhere to sit, and make sure there's shade," Mason orders, before sharing a look with Maverick.

"You stay," Maverick offers. "I'll grab some."

Mason relaxes and takes my arm. I try to shrug him off, but he doesn't budge. I roll my eyes and let him get his way.

"Can you get me a pick n' mix of sweets, and a bottle of Pepsi, please?" Harlow asks, a beaming smile on her face as her gaze bounces from one place to the next, taking it all in.

And I realise, this is the first time she's come to one of our town carnivals.

"You cannot drink Pepsi. You need to try this amazing Slush Puppy. It's to die for. One year, I got brain freeze, and then it started pissing it down with rain, but still, it was worth it for one of their Slush Puppy's," I ramble, then pause when I notice everyone staring at me. I shrug, not even slightly embarrassed. "It was awesome."

"I'll have both," she reveals, smacking her lips together.

My smile dies when Mason's grip tightens, causing me discomfort. I glance over at him, and I'm startled to find his posture rigid and his jaw clenched. His brown eyes are stormy, glaring at something in the distance.

Swallowing past the lump in my throat, I slowly follow his line of sight, and feel my own body grow tense.

It's my turn to squeeze him back. Without thought, I take a step closer to him.

My parents are standing with a group of people, chatting away, but then they both turn, having felt our gazes.

Fuck! Not here. *Not now.*

It's too late. They've noticed me. Mother is throwing me a disgusted look, her lip curled into a snarl.

When I meet my dad's gaze, silently pleading with him to stop her, he looks away, his lips downcast.

"Fuck," I mumble when they start over here.

Dad says something to her, but Mum snaps something back at him, and his shoulders sag. As always, he follows her every command like the good dog he is.

"What are you doing here?" my mother hisses when she reaches us. She grabs my arm and tries to pull me away from the group.

I wince, struggling to get free of her grasp. "Stop!" I demand.

"Let her go, now," Mason growls menacingly.

When she doesn't move quick enough, he grabs her wrist, shoving her away.

"Don't talk to me, you filthy scumbag," she hisses.

I close my eyes, mortified at everyone's reaction. Maverick's jaw is locked, and although Malik looks bored, I know him too well; underneath, he is livid. Harlow's mouth hangs open, but it's Max who draws my attention. He looks ready to burst out laughing.

Now they know.

I tried so hard to keep them away from my friends, and it was for nothing.

"I'll ask again, young lady: what are you doing here?" Mum snaps.

I steel my shoulders and stand tall. "Not that it's any of your business, but I'm staying here for a while. Evan is letting me sleep at his house until the court case is over, then I'll be going back to Nan's."

"Well, at least we have that to be thankful for. But you need to leave. I'm not having you tarnish our name. Go back to Evan's, and don't come back. I will not have people knowing my daughter is a hussy."

Mason growls low in his throat as his hand slides up my arm and over my shoulders. Mum's eyes practically bulge out of their sockets.

"Your daughter is staying here, and she isn't going to be going back to her nan's either. She will be living with me."

Mum scoffs. "I do not think so," she tells him, running her gaze over him with disgust, before turning to me. "I guess I shouldn't be surprised you ended up pregnant if you are hanging out with riff-raff like him."

"Are you going to let her talk to your daughter like that?" Mason barks at my dad.

Dad, looking lost, gazes at me. His forehead wrinkles, and his lips tug down. He opens his mouth to say something, but instead, takes her arm, steering her away. "Come on, Vivian, let's go meet Robert and Darla."

Tears spring to my eyes when I hear his voice. He was my favourite person growing up. But Mum... she ruined him. She sucked the life out of him, and he's barely a shell of the man he once was.

Mum's face reddens, and her body begins to tremble. She pulls away from his touch, not leaving like he requested.

Max laughs and shakes his head, and my mother's attention zones in on him.

"Something funny?" she snarls.

"Yeah, you. You have a brilliant daughter right in front of you. She got good grades, she's polite as fuck to everyone, and hardly ever swears. She lost her virginity to my brother and got up the duff. Worse things could have happened, ya know. She could have come back with an STD or got addicted to drugs," he tells her. I groan at his wording. "If you're going to stand there and look disgusted, go direct your expression at a mirror. That's where the disgust should be aimed."

"How dare you!" she bites out, her eyes narrowing on him. "Charles, dear, are you going to let him talk to me like that?"

Dad steps between them. "Boy, watch your mouth around the lady," he orders, and once again, reaches for Mum's arm. "Come on, Vivian, I can see Darla and Robert over there."

My mother's head whips up, revealing wild eyes that frantically scan the area. I'm not sure if it's because she wants to show off something extravagant she's recently bought, or because she doesn't want to risk them seeing her talking to me. Either way, it pulls her attention away from us.

She scans me one more time, revulsion evident in her expression. "You're an embarrassment," she sneers, before dragging my father away.

I stand there, frozen, and watch them leave. I can't look at the others. *What must they think of me?*

When Harlow speaks, my stomach sinks. They must hate me for her remarks. "Your parents seem really, um… spirited."

The tension is broken with her words. I turn to her, and when she grimaces, I can't help it. I burst into a fit of laughter and give her a look that says, 'no shit'.

"Your mum's a bitch. Whose mum isn't?" Max reveals. "Now, can you get me some food? You guys owe me for eating without me." He pauses when he sees someone in the distance. He smacks Maverick's arm. "Don't forget the extra cheese and mayo. I'll be back."

"Are you okay?" Mason asks once Max is gone. I shrug. I don't know what to say. "Don't let her get to you. She might come around."

I snort. "Or not."

"Or not," he repeats, chuckling.

His posture is still tense as he glances at the crowd my parents blended into.

"I'm sorry for what they said."

"I've heard worse," he admits. Still, he didn't have to be subjected to that behaviour. "C'mon, let's get you that candy floss."

"Alright," I whisper, tears springing to my eyes.

I duck my head, hoping he doesn't see them. I don't want him, or any of them, to know just how much them meeting my parents got to me. I'm ashamed of how they speak to people, and I never wanted my friends to think I was anything like them.

Out of all the things I tried to prepare myself for, bumping into my parents wasn't one of them. It never even crossed my mind. I gave up on them the day they told me to abort the baby or leave.

My nan refuses to give up on my father. She still has hope, and believes if she can get him alone, she can talk to him and make him see reason. What happened in the past doesn't matter to her because she thinks it's only the future that matters. But so far, she hasn't got her chance.

She's fighting a losing battle. She should know by now that Dad doesn't do anything that will go against my mum.

I wish I had parents who cuddled their child when they were in pain, physically or emotionally. But I didn't. My mum doesn't have a motherly bone in her body. The closest she comes to hugging someone is when she gives air kisses to people just like her. She has always been too busy upholding her image to worry about her only daughter.

To her, I was the mistake. I was the one they didn't want. All my life I've had to watch my brother get everything and anything, while I suffered through my mother's continuous criticism. She belittled me every chance she got.

Now, I'm done. Unless I bump into her like I did today, I will never have to hear her cruel words again.

And I'm happy for it to be that way.

CHAPTER
FOUR

DENNY

fter grabbing some food, Mason and I head over to where the group said they'd wait for us. Mason's holding both trays while I carry the bag of drinks and a tub of pink candyfloss.

"Great, you're here. I was starting to think I'd have to make the food myself," Max mumbles unhappily.

"Wouldn't want you to do something that productive now, would we," Maverick sarcastically replies, making us all chuckle.

"At least it would be fucking cheaper. Did you see the price for a meal? Robbing bastards," Mason accuses, his voice rising.

When he reveals the cost for one meal, Max's eyes widen. "I could buy a tin of hotdogs that have eight in a tin, the buns, a bottle of ketchup, and a large bottle of Coke for less than that."

Malik grunts at his brother. "Again, you'd have to cook it yourself, and you don't cook."

"And I don't see it stopping you from eating the food," Mason mutters, curling his lip at his brother, before he shoves half the hotdog in his mouth.

Max quickly chews his food before saying, "Well yeah—because I didn't buy it. You did. Food always tastes better when you don't buy it."

Mason goes to lay into him, so I quickly speak up. "Well, I'll be hungry again soon, so I hope you have some money on you, Max, because the next round is on you," I tell him, rubbing my rounded stomach.

His eyes bulge out. "Trust me, I don't think there's enough food here to fill that," he states, pointing at my stomach.

My lips part in shock at first, but then a laugh slips free. "Cheeky fucker!"

Which brings me to my next dilemma. I'm not sure I'll be able to get down on the blanket graciously.

The nape of my neck tingles, and I turn to find Mason's attention drawn to my stomach. There's a soft smile playing on his lips, a look of hope and want in his eyes.

I close my eyes, summon a deep breath, and hold it in for a second. I don't want to give myself false hope. The novelty of having a baby could wear off within a few days, and he could tell me to leave. I daren't question his expression out loud, but he really does look happy about the baby.

There's a longing in his gaze that wasn't there before. I wish we were alone, so I could ask him what he's thinking.

He shifts his gaze from my stomach to my face, anchoring all my attention. My lips part when his pupils dilate.

He takes a step forward, but stops when Max pipes in. "Are you going to sit down or what? You're making the place look untidy."

Heat rises in my cheeks as the spell Mason has me under is broken. From the looks on everyone else's faces, they saw the little stare-off we were having.

Flustered, I wave him off. "I'll, um, I need to find…" I pause, scanning the park for an unoccupied bench, but they're all filled with families.

Mason's eyebrows scrunch together as he moves closer. "What's wrong?"

Letting out a sigh, I explain. "If I do manage to get down there, I don't think I'll be able to get back up."

Realisation dawns, and he lets out a chuckle. "Come here." He holds his hands out to me, and I take them, using his strength to lower myself down onto the blanket.

Once seated, my bladder protests. It's going to be a nightmare for everyone involved with me having to get up every two minutes for the loo.

A man speaking through a microphone clears his throat, gaining everyone's attention. "Ladies and gentlemen, today we have a local tribute band up first. Please welcome... Mini Mix!"

Five girls around fifteen skip on stage, diving straight into *Wings* by Little Mix . I flipping love that band. I spent thirty quid on the night of the *X-Factor* finals for them to win. My favourite song of theirs is *Little Me*. It's soulful, truthful, and so beautiful.

"I love this song," I cry out. Chuckles sound around me at my excitement.

"You love all songs," Max fires back. "I'm still making Liam pay for leaving you in charge of the playlist at his party."

"Hey, *Living on a Prayer* is the tune, my man." I tut, scowling at him.

Max has always had an issue with the music I listen to. Has since the night I put *Living on a Prayer* on at Liam's party. Then again when he caught me singing, *I Need a Hero* by Bonnie Tyler, on the karaoke. He literally laughed in my face.

"You said the same thing about Miley Cyrus's song *Wrecking ball*—until you watched the video for it, and said it put you off the song," Mason pipes in.

I turn to him, my eyebrows hitting my hairline. I can't believe he remembers me telling him that. Butterflies erupt in my stomach at how sweet it is.

I hate that I'm already getting used to his presence again. I don't want to, but it's hard when he has this way about him. I want to say something sassy back, to tease him, but thankfully, *Move* begins to play. I squeal and sing along to the words whilst moving my hips.

A sharp kick near my belly button has me bending forward. I

clutch my stomach, inhaling sharply when baby kicks again, up against my rib.

Shit, that one hurt, little man.

"Are you okay? What's wrong? Is it the baby?" Mason rushes out, kneeling next to me.

I grip his hand, squeezing as the baby kicks again.

Someone is awake today.

I straighten when the next one doesn't hurt as much, and go to assure Mason I'm okay, but I'm taken aback when I find everyone crowded around, all on their knees.

My lips part as I stare up at Mason, who has gone as pale as a ghost.

"I'm—" I inhale at another kick, so instead of trying to tell him, I show him. I reach for his hand, ignoring the sparks that zap between us, and place it over my lower stomach. The baby kicks right under his palm, and I let out a chuckle.

Mason's head snaps up to meet my gaze. He looks bewildered and in complete awe. I give him a smile, knowing exactly how he's feeling right now.

At first, I didn't know what the flutters were, but then the midwife explained it was the baby moving. From there, I became obsessed with wanting to feel him or her move. The first time I felt the real force of a kick, it turned my world upside down. It was the day everything became real for me.

"Does it hurt?" he whispers, his eyes drifting away from where his hand is resting on my stomach.

When his gaze reaches mine, I find his eyes brimmed with tears, and it takes everything in me not to crawl into his lap.

"No," I whisper back, too lost in the moment. So lost that when I hear Maverick's voice sounding rather close to me, I jump.

"Can I feel?" he asks hesitantly.

Maverick is the eldest of the brothers, so he's the only one I don't really know all that well. And the request coming from someone so badass kind of surprises me. He's the largest of the Carter's, and the quietest. I remember thinking he was rude when I first met him, but once I realised he wasn't, and that he had a lot of responsibility on his shoulders and a pain hidden beneath his façade, I warmed to him.

Mason tenses beside me when I reach for Maverick's hand, nodding. His grin changes his whole appearance.

Mason, however, doesn't feel as comfortable as I do because he refuses to remove his hand. I melt at his behaviour. Tough, rugged, man-whore Mason is whipped by his unborn baby. It isn't a fake reaction. It's real. And right now, he doesn't want to share he or she with anyone else.

"Mason, Maverick wants to feel," I whisper, my lips twitching.

Mason gives Maverick a warning glare before reluctantly removing his hand.

"Not for long," Mason orders, keeping his voice low like he doesn't want to disturb the baby.

Placing Maverick's hand on my bump, I smile at him encouragingly. He startles when the baby kicks my stomach hard, making me wince for a second. He chuckles, mesmerised at my bump.

"Definitely a boy," he announces, beaming like a proud uncle. "It feels like he's playing football in there."

"I wouldn't know—*you're* hogging the belly," Mason grumbles, which I find amusing.

"I need to feel this," Harlow says, crawling over the blankets to us. Mason grunts beside me, not sounding very impressed. I just roll my eyes at him and nod at Harlow.

Her reaction is the same as Maverick's, except her eyes water as she tells me how incredible it feels.

"Malik, you need to feel this," she gushes, but he shakes his head, his face scrunched up in horror. "Don't be a baby."

She nearly pulls his arm out of its socket when she grabs his hand and drags him over the blanket, before placing it on my stomach.

My lips twitch at his expression. "Holy fucking hell. It didn't seem real until this moment. There really is a baby inside there."

"What—did you think I'd just gotten fat or something?" I ask, pretending to be hurt.

"Malik," Mason snaps at his younger brother.

Myles goes next, murmuring, "Awesome," when he feels the kick.

The only person who hasn't felt him move is Max, and he's been uncharacteristically quiet. His gaze is firmly fixed on my belly. Or my chest. It could be either. But there's a hesitancy there that the others didn't have.

"Want to feel?" I ask him.

"I don't think Mason would appreciate me feeling his girlfriend up in public," he replies, winking.

The word 'girlfriend' has me tensing, before I remind myself not to get worked up over it. Mason growls and curses at him under his breath, but I force a smile, not letting them know it got to me.

"Come here, pleb-head," I order, reaching for Max's hand.

He slides across the blanket to get closer, placing his hand in the same place the others did, but this time, nothing happens.

"I don't feel anything," he murmurs, sounding disappointed.

"Hold on." I poke my stomach, trying to wake the baby back up. All of a sudden, the baby fully turns, and Max flies backwards, his face pale as he stares at my stomach with a horrified expression.

"That's a fucking alien," he screeches, looking a little green. "I knew it would be half alien anyway coming from my brother and all, but holy shit, that felt really weird. Did that hurt? Was that a kick? I saw your stomach doing the Mexican wave," he rambles, his voice high-pitched.

"No, that was definitely not a kick. He or she moved position."

"Doesn't that hurt?" Mason asks, and I shake my head. The only time it really hurts is when I'm startled by a kick or get a kick to the bladder. The rest just feels foreign to me.

"That was amazing," Harlow announces. "Hey, I need to get some new photos. Say cheese."

Maverick and Mason lean in closer, clearly used to Harlow's photo fetish. I, however, don't get a chance to smile or say cheese before she's snapping the photo, taking me off guard.

Great! I'm going to look like one of the hillbillies off 'The Hills Have Eyes' while Mason and Maverick are going to look like something out of 'Magic Mike'. It's unfair.

———

Today has been a good day. We spent it watching other acts come up on stage. Some were good, some were horrible, but even those were entertaining. I laughed all afternoon.
I think my favourite part wasn't the show or the food or candyfloss, but spending time with my friends. I've missed them like crazy.

Once I left, I assumed it would kill what friendship we did have, but I was wrong. If anything, our friendship is stronger. They've all welcomed me back, and not once has anyone made a sly comment or begrudged me for leaving. And they had every right to since I kept the baby hidden from Mason.

The day is coming to an end, and we'll be leaving soon to get back. It's getting too crowded, and now all the families are leaving, it's getting louder and more boisterous. More people have arrived in their wake, but it's mostly teenagers and younger adults who want to get drunk and party. The beer stands are now open, which isn't good for us since we're sitting on the ground. We've already had two drunken lads' trip over a bag next to us. I knew Mason was about to lose it, so I was taken aback when he listened to me to leave it.

Although I don't want the day to end, the heat is beginning to get to me. We moved to the shade a few times, but that only lasted twenty minutes or so before we were engulfed in sun again. I gave up in the end, assuring them I was fine.

I wasn't. I have under-boob sweat and my thighs are sticking together. It isn't healthy, and right now, I feel like a sweaty whale, or what I imagine a sweaty whale to look like.

Fanning myself with a leaflet some pizza guy left with us, I lean against the pillow Maverick made from the spare blanket to shove against the tree for me to lean back on.

It has been like this all day. They've been so attentive and caring. Knowing they want to be in the baby's life warms my heart.

"Are you hungry again?" Max moans when he sees me rub my belly.

Seriously, I've eaten four times since we got here. Two of those times were just to get Max to spend his money after his comment about Mason buying him expensive food. I almost laugh at his disgruntled expression.

"Believe it or not, Max, I'm not," I reply, laughing when his shoulders sag.

"Thank the Lord. I'm down to my last tenner," he explains, groaning.

"Oh, so you've got enough to get me some more candyfloss before we go?" I half joke. I've been dying to buy another tub, but I felt embarrassed with all the food I'd consumed.

Max opens his mouth, but it's not his voice I hear. "Don't you think you've had enough food?" a sweet yet bitter voice remarks.

I groan at the group of girls who stop around our circle. I remember them from school. I loathed each and every one of them.

They're ogling the Carter brothers, and although I don't blame them, it still has my back up.

"Nah, I could totally go to KFC and I'd still probably enjoy a Subway after," I reply sweetly. "Thanks for caring though, Aimee."

"Okaaay," she replies, rolling her eyes. She turns her beady gaze to Mason, and her grim smile spreads into a seductive smirk. "Hi Mason."

I knew this would happen. This is what I was afraid of.

My fingernails dig into the palms of my hands, which are ready to strike if Mason even thinks of flirting back in front of me right now. I have no claim to him, but I'm not going to sit here and watch it; not anymore.

He might not want me, but I deserve a little more respect than what he has given me.

When he grunts his acknowledgement, I give her a triumphant smirk, feeling a little smug. He isn't forcing himself not to speak to her; he genuinely doesn't want to. When he moves closer, his gaze still focussed on my stomach, I smile. He has been waiting for the baby to move again, despite me telling him he or she is asleep.

Aimee loses her smirk and glares at me. If I could do a happy dance right now, I would. I love how much I've gotten to her.

She still doesn't leave. Instead, she pulls her top down further, showing more of her cleavage.

"A few of us are going to Heaven tonight. Mase, you should come. We can go back to mine after and…" she trails off, twirling a piece of hair around her finger.

"Is he going to kick?" Mason asks, rubbing his hand over my stomach.

I don't think he heard her, and although it shouldn't, that makes me happy.

"Sorry, he's going to be busy with me," I tell her sweetly, throwing in a wink to piss her off.

The girl stomps her foot, and her friends follow her cue and send me glares of their own. I just smile sweetly, but nearly choke on air when I hear Harlow mutter under her breath.

"Somebody give the girl a brain."

Malik sniggers, not caring about expressing his amusement. When the girls glower down at him, he shoves his face into the crook of Harlow's neck, howling with laughter.

"Girls, as boring as it's been seeing you, you're blocking the last bit of light," Max states, shooing them away with his hand from where he's lying on the grass sunbathing, his eyes remaining closed.

"Call me if you change your mind. My number is—"

"Are you serious, Aimee? Back off. You can see he's not interested, so run along with your little friends and leave us alone," I snap, wishing I wasn't stuck on the ground right now.

"Whatever, bitch," she sneers, and then pales when Mason finally looks away from my stomach.

"Leave," he growls.

She storms off with her friends trailing behind her. As soon as they're out of sight, Mason's shoulders slump, and his body relaxes. His eyes are filled with remorse when he turns his attention to me.

"I'm sorry," he murmurs.

"Please tell me you've never been with her?" I ask, my heart stopping at the thought he might say yes.

He looks taken aback, his face reddening. "What? No. She tried to get into the club a few times, but I always sent her away. I know my reputation isn't clean cut, but I do have some standards."

"Of course you do," I reply patronisingly, tapping his head. "You slept with me."

A slow smirk curves his lips. "True. And what will we be busy doing tonight?"

The breath leaves my lungs in a whoosh, and I find myself unable to look away. "Mason," I murmur, hoping he didn't read too much into my earlier comment. I just wanted her to leave.

"It's fine," he tells me, the arrogance leaving his smirk.

Maverick stands, wiping the grass from his jeans and hands. He'd been leaning back on his hands, enjoying the show.

"I need to get going, guys. Does anyone need a lift?" he asks, giving Max a pointed look.

"Nope. I'm going to get me some pussy. I'll see you guys later," he reveals, and holds his hand up in front of me for a high-five. He's grinning like a fool. "Let me know when you're ready to tell Mason the kid is mine."

Mason growls, and Max hightails it out of there. Mason looks ready to run after him. Thankfully, he doesn't. "Prick," he grunts.

"We'll get a lift from you. We need to get back," Malik answers, and I turn to look at Harlow. Her face is flushed, and immediately I know why they need to get back. I roll my eyes.

Maverick does the same but adds in a groan.

Mason helps me to my feet, refusing to let me help clear the stuff away or even carry something back to the car.

His gestures—although frustrating—are kind of sweet.

And I have to wonder: will this behaviour last?

CHAPTER FIVE

DENNY

hen we arrive at my brother's place, Lexi is standing outside the front door, looking all dressed up. Her purple maxi dress clings to her curves in all the right places. It was styled to be sexy yet casual, and she's working both.

It makes me wonder if there's more than just friendship between her and my brother.

Mason shuts off the car, and I turn to him whilst undoing my seat-belt. "Thank you for today. I've had so much fun," I admit, smiling. I lose my smile when he undoes his own seatbelt. "Um, what are you doing?"

"I'm coming in for a bit. We really need to talk, Denny. I know we've not had the chance to yet, but I can't let it keep hanging in the air. We have things to plan, and the scan is on Friday. I want things between us to be cleared up, or at the very least, for us to be on the same page. Please, give me a chance to talk," he pleads, looking utterly lost.

I sag against the seat, giving him a nod. "You're right, we should."

Pushing open the door, I exit the car and search my bag for the keys. I'm starting to lose faith I'll find them, when my fingers touch the metal key. I refrain myself from fist pumping the air and shouting, 'got them'.

Lexi stops pacing the walkway, her face pale when she spots me. I forgot she was there, having been distracted by Mason.

"Hey, Lexi," I greet, giving her a small wave.

She forces a smile, fiddling with her fingers. "Hey, Denny. Can I talk to you for a second? Alone?" Her gaze flicks to Mason briefly before returning to me.

"Sure," I agree, handing the keys to Mason. "Why don't you go put the kettle on? Everything is in there."

He watches Lexi for a moment, looking apprehensive about leaving me. "Maybe I should—" he starts, but I cut him off.

"Go. I'll stay out here by the door," I tell him, rolling my eyes.

He doesn't move for a moment, seeming to be at war with himself. I inwardly grin when his shoulders sag and he lets out a sigh, knowing I've won.

"Okay. Five minutes. We really do need to talk," he reminds me.

"I know."

I wait until he's unlocked the door before turning to Lexi. "Is everything okay?"

She tucks a strand of hair behind her ear. "Have you spoken with Evan at all?"

"No, why?" I ask, dread filling my stomach. "Is there something I should know?"

"I really don't want to worry you," she begins, her hands shaking. "But he usually calls me by now and he hasn't. I'm worried. It's not like him to not call. I'm going out of my mind." She takes a breath, forcing out a laugh. "I hoped it was him who turned up after you left this afternoon, but it wasn't. It was just some guy dropping a letter or something off. I did come out to see if he knew anything, but he was already in the car by the time I made it outside," she rambles, pacing again.

"Have you tried calling him?" I ask softly.

"Yes. A lot. If he can't answer, he always calls back," she explains.

I can see the deep concern, but I feel like I'm missing something.

"I'm sorry if I'm overstepping, but I'm confused and just want to understand. Is there something going on between you and my brother? If there is, I swear, he wouldn't cheat. He's probably just busy," I assure her.

The truth is, Evan is a man whore who sleeps with anyone with a vagina. But I know for a fact he wouldn't go into a relationship to cheat on someone and cause them unnecessary pain. He is brutal with his honesty and would end it before he ever cheated.

Telling Lexi that… well, it would only cause her heartache and break them up. I can't do that.

"What? God no! I just… I, um—"

"It's okay. I'm not judging," I tell her, holding my hands up.

She chews on her lower lip, looking unsure and slightly shaken still.

"No, it's not that," she blurts out, taking a step back and running a hand through her hair. "We aren't a couple or anything. There's nothing sexual between us." She takes a deep breath, squaring her shoulders. "Did he say anything to you about me?"

"I'm sorry, no."

She nods like that's okay, then turns to me, her eyes pleading. "What I'm about to tell you can't go any further. You need to promise me."

I step closer, keeping my voice low. "I swear, I'll keep it to myself," I promise, hoping my brother hasn't put himself in danger. It wouldn't be the first time.

"Your brother… he saved me. I was in an abusive relationship, and it was escalating. He got me out of there. If it wasn't for him, I'd be dead right now. He let me move in next door for free, offering me protection in case my ex ever found me. It might seem silly, but he helps with the anxiety. He checks in with me when he's away working. He's the only real friend I've got."

"And he hasn't called," I finish, feeling bad for blowing her off.

"I'm probably overreacting and he's busy, but I just have a bad feeling."

"If there's one thing I know about my brother, it's that he can take care of himself. I'm sure he'll call once he has a chance."

"Yeah," she murmurs, still looking lost.

"What if I try calling him in a bit to see if he answers. I'll be honest, I've called him a few times, but he hasn't answered, so I wouldn't hold your breath. If he does though, I'll get him to call you."

Her entire body sags, a real smile spreading across her face. "Thank you, Denny. I'm sorry if I've worried you. It's just not like him."

I genuinely feel sorry for her. She's clearly been through enough, and if my brother has been her saviour, no wonder she's out of sorts. "No, I'm glad you came to me. I wish I could help more. But I promise, if something happened, I would have been called."

She nods, although she still doesn't seem convinced. "I'll let you get back to your friend," she tells me.

"Alright. Take care, Lexi. I hope he calls you back soon," I tell her.

"And you'll let me know if he calls?"

"I promise."

Satisfied, she gives me a nod before escaping back into her house. I turn to head inside and startle when I find Mason standing in the doorway, his muscled arms crossed over his large, sculpted chest. His gaze narrows on Lexi's retreating back.

"What did she want?" he growls.

I roll my eyes. "Jesus, gossip much?"

"She basically just dismissed me like I don't have feelings. *That* really hurt my feelings, angel."

I laugh at his lame attempt to look miserable. His eyelids droop and his lips pull down into a sad pout.

"Poor, Mason," I tease, stepping inside. "She was just asking if I had any spare tampons left, but…" I point down to my large stomach, grinning when Mason turns green. "I'm kidding."

"Yeah. I knew that," he mutters, shaking his head.

He takes my hands, guides me over to the sofa, and helps me take a seat. I knew this moment would come, and I don't want to torture myself any longer.

"So, you wanted to talk," I begin when he takes a seat on the edge of the coffee table.

"Yeah," he confirms, looking at me intensely. "I really think you should move in with me, Denny. I want you to. I know I've been a jerk, but I can make this right. This baby deserves us to try."

He couldn't be more wrong.

"No, they don't. You met my parents, Mason. I grew up in a cold, lonely home. I don't want that for our baby. I want them to be loved, and they won't feel that if we are at each other's throats all the time. It's one of the reasons why I was so scared to tell you. You made it adamantly clear you didn't want to be with me, so it could have gone either of two ways. One, you would have changed your entire life and got back with me out of obligation because you wanted to do the right thing, or you would have asked me to get rid of him. Either choice didn't sit well with me."

"Her!"

"Her?" I question, confused.

"Yes, her. The baby is going to be a she," he explains, and my lips twitch at how confident he sounds. "What you need to understand, Denny, is if you had told me back then, I'd be saying the same things I am right now. I want to give us a try."

"Mason, you couldn't stand the sight of me. Now you want something to do with me *because* of the baby. I don't want that, Mason. I want someone to love *me*, to cherish *me*, and believe it or not, be happy to be with me. I don't want you to feel forced into a relationship you clearly didn't want a few months ago," I tell him, my throat clogging with emotion when old feelings begin to resurface.

He shakes his head. "You really don't get it, do you? I've wanted you for years. I'm older, Denny, and I liked you when you started high school, even though it felt wrong. And then we grew close, and I couldn't... Those feelings never changed."

"Well, you freaking out then kicking me out after we slept together said otherwise," I snap, my bottom lip trembling. "So did the millions of girls you had afterwards."

"I was a dickhead, Denny. You might not believe me, but that night was the best night of my life. You were still sleeping when I woke up. I remember looking at you and thinking how peaceful and innocent you looked. Your lips were swollen from kissing, your cheeks were still flushed, and your hair was spread out over my pillow. It hurt just watching you," he reveals, taking a breath. "When I saw the blood on the sheets, it all hit me at once. I'd just taken your innocence. I felt like I was turning into my dad, and I couldn't do that to you. Couldn't bear it. That night, we didn't make any promises to each other, but I felt that everything was said with our actions, and then everything... Everything went to shit. I honestly thought pushing you away was what was best for you at the time. I didn't want you to end up with a waste of space like me."

I can hear the truth in his words. I only know a little about their dad, so hearing him open up, it's gutting me.

"Then why did you break my heart, Mase? You kept throwing girls in my face, knowing it was tearing me up inside. You watched me suffer and did nothing. You hurt me with the words you spoke that morning, and they continued to hurt me every night in my dreams. They haunted me."

I can't look away from him, not even when the tears begin to fall.

"I didn't sleep with them," he whispers, looking ashamed as he ducks his head.

He has been truthful up until this point. What makes me angry is that I was starting to forgive him.

I grit my teeth. "Don't lie to me, Mason. I saw you with more than one girl. The first time I went to tell you about the baby, you were walking arm in arm with a girl and completely ignored me. You looked right through me. But I kept trying, Mason. I even tried the day I left with Nan, and another random girl answered your door and said you were busy."

There is one thing I hate more than cheats and bullies, and that's liars. All he had to do was tell the truth. If he wants a go at this, the least he could do is take responsibility for his actions.

"What you saw was what you wanted to see; what I needed you to see. If you had tried to talk to me, or beg me to take a chance on you just once, I would have surrendered and done anything you wanted. But you didn't. You can place all the blame on me, but, Denny, you didn't fight for me either." He takes a deep breath after hitting me with the truth. "I never slept with any of those girls."

"What? I... I don't... What?" I shake my head, not believing what I'm hearing. It all feels too much. I rub at my chest above my heart, trying to ease the ache there.

"I made it look like I was sleeping around. All of them tried. One night, I was fed up of wanting you and not having you, so I tried to fuck one of them. But I couldn't. She didn't compare to you. It was then that I started hating myself more. I had wanted you for so long." He forces out a dry laugh. "I dreamed about wanting you all the time, and then I had you, and fucked it up. I couldn't forget you, no matter how hard I tried, because there is no other you. I'm so fucking sorry for what I did. You'll never realise how much."

I'm rocked by the revelation. I don't know what to believe. I feel like my world is turning upside down for the third time, and I can't catch my breath.

"I feel so lost right now. How am I supposed to believe you never slept with any of them? What about the girl at the racetrack? The one Davis blackmailed to sleep with you?"

"She was the only one I got close to sleeping with, Denny, and believe me, I only did it because when I looked at you—when I saw how much you hated me—I couldn't handle it. I needed to erase that look from my mind. I got wasted that night; but it wore off as soon as her mouth was around my cock."

"I don't want to know specifics, Mason. Christ!" I cry, standing up.

"Shit! Sorry. I just need you to understand, Denny. I never did what you think I did, and it's not an excuse because I know it still caused you pain."

"You're right. It hurt me because everything you did *was* real to me.

I didn't fight for you, Mason, because you gave me nothing to fight for. You made it clear. It was why I couldn't talk to anyone about the baby. I felt humiliated because of your actions. Harlow was with your brother, and I knew she would tell him. I couldn't confide in anyone.

"You treated me like I was a kid after we slept together. I couldn't get that out of my head. Then I kept running through scenarios about telling you. Would you tell me to get rid of the baby? Would you accuse me of trapping you? I couldn't go through that humiliation again. It hurt enough when the women would brag about being with you.

"Even with all the pain you caused, I still didn't want to be the person who forced you to be someone you aren't. You made it clear what you wanted, and it wasn't me. So I left. I knew Harlow would tell you that night, so I changed my number and didn't tell her where we were going." I let out a breath, my throat clogged with emotion as he sits there and listens. "I have been so scared and alone. When that letter arrived, summoning me to court to testify, I panicked. My chest felt tight like I couldn't breathe, all because I still didn't want to hurt you. No matter what you did, I still couldn't hurt you, and I didn't want you to hate me."

He rubs my knee, his mouth tight. "Denny—"

I wipe the tears from my cheeks. "I was so scared of coming back here. I was petrified you and your family would hate me for not getting an abortion," I cry out. I place my hand over my stomach protectively.

"Denny," he croaks out as kneels in front of me. He places his hands over my stomach, where mine are. His eyes glisten with tears when he looks up at me. "I would never have asked you to abort the baby. *Ever.* I tried my hardest to get Harlow to give me your new number, to tell me where you lived, because I wanted to talk to you. When she said you refused to talk about the baby or me, I went out of my mind. I was scared to death I'd never see you again, or that you would abort the baby *because* of everything I had done. I had no way of knowing what you had done, not until you stepped off the train. I couldn't believe it when I saw your bump."

My heart clenches, and I place my hands over his, feeling his pain as if it was my own. "If you didn't know, why would you have planned for us to move in together?"

A light pink tinge rises in his cheeks. "Because I knew I couldn't lose you again. No matter what the situation was going to be, I knew I was going to earn your forgiveness."

"But Mark mentioned a baby's room," I murmur, trying to wrap my head around what he's saying.

He exhales, rubbing a hand over his jaw. "Because despite that 'what if', I knew you, Denny. I knew you wouldn't do that, no matter who the father was. You have a heart of gold. You would have still loved this baby with everything in you." He presses closer, his chest rubbing against my knees. "We can do this. I know I messed up, and I know what I did was unforgiveable, but we can get through this. We can."

I tilt my head, not bothering to wipe the tears away. "What if we can't? What if you change your mind and I wake up one day to find you've moved on. I can't go through that again. I can't."

My breath hitches as he leans forward, wiping under my eyes. "Move in with me. Let me show you how wrong you are; let me show you how good we are together and how sorry I am. I never meant to hurt you. I was trying to prevent that from happening, and I ended up hurting you anyway. It's not going to happen again," he pleads, placing his hands back over my stomach.

The baby decides to kick at that moment, as if he's agreeing with his dad. Mason's gaze goes to my stomach, and love and awe fill his expression as he smiles.

I let him share the moment, content in watching him watch my stomach. When he looks up, he arches an cyebiow.

"I don't know what to do," I whisper honestly.

I don't want him to hurt me again. He's been all I've ever wanted since I first laid eyes on him. I saved myself, hoping that one day he would see me. The day he did, I felt like I was walking on cloud nine.

They are always telling you to make sure you pick the right one for your first because it will be the one you remember for the rest of your life. And they're right. Because there is no way I'll ever forget him.

Before I really got to know him, I remember telling people I wouldn't care if he only wanted one night because I'd give it to him. Back then, I'd have done anything to be one of the girls he had on his arm.

Then I got to know him, and I didn't just want more, I wanted everything. He owned me that night. I never imagined my first time would be as beautiful and amazing as it was. Even now, I don't think anything could compare to that night.

"Will you at least think about it?" he asks, his lips tipped down.

I nod. "Yes. Yes, I will."

When he moves away, removing his hands from my stomach, I want to protest and put his hands back where they were.

"I'm going to get going and let you get some rest. It's getting late."

"Okay," I reply, getting up to see him out.

He stops at the door, turning to face me. "Call me if you need anything, no matter what time it is."

"I will. I promise."

He tucks a strand of hair behind my ear. "Please think about what I said."

I swallow past the lump in my throat. "I will."

"See you tomorrow," he replies, yet he doesn't move.

He shakes his head, gives me and my stomach one last glance, before leaving, heading down the path.

I lock up behind him, a yawn escaping me. I hadn't realised how tired I was until now. With the sun and food, I'm knackered and too tired to unpack again. But not too tired to go grab a shower to wash away the sweat and grime from today.

After finishing up in the bathroom, I head into my bedroom with a towel wrapped around me. Seeing the curtains still wide open, I walk over to shut them. I grab the cream material, pushing it closed, when something across the street startles me. I jump back at seeing the silhouette of a person leaning against a tree.

With my heart racing, I quickly rush back to the window, scanning the street. When I see it's gone, I sag against the frame, letting out a sigh as I rub my tired eyes. The day has caught up with me. I'm not surprised I'm starting to see things.

Still, even as I shut the curtains closed, that feeling you get when someone is watching you, has awareness tingling up my spine.

CHAPTER
SIX

DENNY

I t's Friday, the day I get to find out the sex of the baby. I'm beyond excited. The anticipation made last night hard for me to sleep.

I'm finally going to find out if I'm having a boy or a girl.

I know there are other things they have to do at my appointment, like take bloods and measurements. As long as the baby is okay and healthy, they can do what they need to. I kind of feel guilty for not going to an appointment sooner in case something is wrong. It's why I made the appointment for the scan to begin with.

My feet had swollen to the point I couldn't wear shoes anymore—only my flip-flops. And I remembered reading in a magazine Nan had given me that swollen feet were listed among potential dangers during pregnancy, so I went to the doctors, scared out of my mind. Luckily, the doctors weren't worried and told me to elevate them. It was then that I scheduled today's appointment, so that if they were still swollen, I could tell the doctor I'm seeing today.

Thinking of my nan brings up the memory of our phone call last night. She's been calling every day since I arrived to check in on me, but I avoided going into anything more than how me and the baby were feeling. Last night, however, I broke and told her everything. I told her what Mason said and what he's done for me. I had been so scared she'd give me the third degree and another lecture, but she surprised me by telling me to give him a chance.

"Are you trying to get rid of me?" I asked.

"Never, child. But I have a good feeling about him. About you. This baby deserves you both to at least try."

She was right. I know what it's like to grow up in a cold home. My mum used to show me off, so she could brag to her friends her kid was cleverer than theirs, and more beautiful. She wanted a child she could show off when the timing suited her, but in reality, she couldn't stand the sight of me. But I often wondered how we could have been if she wasn't so cold.

My baby won't have to wonder what if. No matter what happens between me and Mason, our child will be loved. They won't be a trophy, or a tool to be used. Neither Mason nor I will allow it, and I truly believe we both want the best for our child.

There's a light knock on the door, and I pull myself away from my thoughts and head over to it. I pull open the door and greet Mason with a smile. Today, he's wearing a pair of cargo shorts, a white short-sleeved T-shirt, and a cap he has put on backwards. I sigh dreamily at the muscle of hotness.

"Hey," I greet.

He smiles, whistling through his teeth as his gaze runs over my body. "You look beautiful."

My cheeks heat at the compliment. "Thank you."

"Are you ready? We've got about twenty minutes to get there."

"Yep. Let me just go grab my bag," I tell him and rush down to the room I'm staying in.

When I step into the room, I'm greeted by cool air breezing through the window. My head snaps in the direction of the window, seeing it open.

I didn't open that.

Or at least, I'm pretty sure I didn't.

No, I know I didn't. With the heat being insufferable, I have been leaving the ceiling fan on. But for it to work, the windows have to be shut, otherwise it just blows out hot air, making it worse.

Plus, I'm petrified of moths. I hate them. They aren't like flies, which fly off at the slightest movement or noise. They have no boundaries at all. After waking up to one that kept landing on my face, I've slept with the window shut ever since.

A shiver runs through me as I step up to the window, my gaze automatically going to the place I saw the silhouette a few nights ago. I know I'm being paranoid when there is nothing there. But still… I can't wash away this feeling that someone is watching me.

"Denny? You okay?" Mason yells, shaking me from my thoughts.

"Yeah," I call back, slamming the window shut.

I meet him back by the front door, giving him a small smile.

"You okay?" he asks, watching me closely.

I wave off his concern. "Yeah. Baby brain is all. The window was open. I must've forgotten I opened it," I explain, shrugging off my anxiety.

Mason doesn't look convinced though. "I don't like that you're staying here on your own," he admits. "Have you thought any more about moving into the new place? Joan and Harlow helped decorate it. They seemed to know what you'd like, so the only room left to do is the baby's room, but I wanted to confirm she's a girl before we did anything, and get your input."

"Boy," I remark, smiling.

"Girl."

"Optimistic today, aren't you," I half tease as he pulls open the passenger side door to his car.

Helping me in, he then bends down, winking. "Yep, and I've already got the pink paint in the shed, ready for when we get back."

When he's in the car, I wait for him to pull his seatbelt on before speaking. "I wasn't just talking about the sex of the baby, but about me moving in."

"I know," he tells me, letting out a sigh. "I just didn't want to make you mad by going on about it. Moving in needs to be your decision, not mine. I'd never force you into something you didn't want, just like you wouldn't do to me. I really want this with you, Denny; I don't want to fuck it up by being controlling and overbearing. I think you've spent your entire life being controlled."

Damn him and his easy charm.

My stomach flutters with butterflies, and it's not because of the baby. It's his words. He's making it hard for me to resist him. I want to take this step with him, to be a family. I know I'm stalling the inevitable, but before I make any more big decisions, I want to be sure this is truly going to work.

You're having a baby together. You can't get more committed than that.

I shake away my thoughts and turn to stare out the window, watching the scenery pass by.

———

W e arrive at the hospital with five minutes to spare. It gives us a chance to sign in and take a seat in the waiting area.

Mason's leg bounces as he runs his hands down his thighs. I place my hand over his leg, stopping the bouncing. "Stop worrying."

"I can't help it," he admits, giving me a sheepish smile.

A small red-headed woman with soft features steps out into the waiting area. "Denny Smith?"

"That's me," I call out, grabbing my bag before letting Mason help me to my feet. He pauses, unsure of what to do. "You okay?"

"Um, I didn't ask, but, um, I can come in, right?"

Chuckling under my breath, I nod. "Of course."

"Great," he croaks out, nearly tripping over a wooden table piled with magazines. He straightens the table, looking up and grimacing. "Sorry."

I grab his hand and pull him down the hall, to where the nurse is waiting. "This way."

The room is dimly lit, giving it a warm and relaxing atmosphere. I take in all the equipment, my stomach fluttering when I spot the ultra-sound. Now that I'm here, I'm even more excited. It's really happening. When I leave this hospital, I will know if I'm having a son or a daughter.

The nurse pulls down a fresh blue sheet across the bed. "Can you lie down on the bed for us and lift up your dress?" she asks, before handing me a small blanket. "You can use this to cover your bottom half."

"Thank you," I tell her, fiddling with the blanket.

When she reaches for more blue roll, my eyebrows pull together. "Here. If you tuck it in the waistband of your knickers, it will stop the gel from getting on your clothing and becoming sticky. I do it with all the mums who come through."

She pulls the curtain across, giving me privacy. I turn to Mason, who shrugs, his gaze going to the bed. "Here, let me help."

I let him help me up on the bed and lie back against the pillows, my cheeks flaming when he pushes my dress up.

He clears his throat, taking his gaze off my knickers, and places the blanket over my legs. When his fingers brush over my stomach, tucking the paper towel into the waistband of my knickers, I have to bite my lip to stifle a moan.

Oh God.

He glances up, his eyes heated when he stares at me.

"Are you decent?" the nurse asks.

Mason jumps away from me, straightening. I clear my throat. "Yes."

"You can take a seat, Dad. You might be here awhile," she explains, and like a puppet being controlled, he drops into the seat, taking in all the machinery.

"It's going to be okay."

His wild gaze meets mine, and he jerks a nod. "Yeah. I'm just…"

"Nervous," I finish, before admitting, "I was too when I had my dating scan."

"You'll have Mr. Harris performing the scan today. He should be here—" She pauses when the door suddenly opens. A burly man with a large stomach enters, his blue scrubs loose on his body. "Ah, here he is."

He pushes his glasses up his nose, smiling in greeting. "Hi, I'm Mr. Harris. I'll be doing your scan today. I've just been going over the notes from your midwife. Can you give me your name, date of birth, and address, please?"

He takes the seat next to me in front of the ultrasound machine, listening as I answer all his questions.

Mason leans against the bed when Mr Harris flicks the machine on, typing in a series of commands.

I close my eyes, and suddenly, all the excitement disappears and I become restless and nervous. What if there is something wrong with the baby? What if I have risked our baby's health by not coming sooner?

I place my hand over my stomach, which turns out to be a mistake when my bladder begins screaming for me to go relieve myself. And now my mind is on my bladder, I can't stop thinking about how badly I need to pee.

Thoughts race through my mind, until he turns, a bottle of gel in his hand.

"Are you ready to see your baby?" Mr Harris asks.

Without thought, I reach for Mason's hand and squeeze it gently. "Yes," I whisper as Mason gulps beside me.

"This may be cold, so be prepared," he warns, and I inwardly groan.

I tense as the pressure in my bladder becomes unbearable. I'm going to piss myself in front of Mason. I'm never going to live it down.

The cold gel hits my stomach, and to my own relief, I don't wet myself. My relief is short-lived when he presses the handheld machine onto my belly, right under my bump, where it presses down on my bladder.

Yep, I think I'm losing fluid. Great! This is just great!

I wiggle, feeling uncomfortable. The doctor—or whatever he's called in his line of work—notices, and gives me a reassuring smile.

"I'll just take the measurements and what I need as quickly as I can. Then the bathroom is right through there," he explains, jerking his head to the door behind Mason.

Mason glances from the monitor to me, his eyebrows pulled together. "What's going on? Is everything okay?"

"I think I drank too much water and I'm kinda struggling not to pee myself," I admit, trying not to giggle when his mouth falls open.

"Oh," he murmurs, but his attention falls behind me, to the sound coming from the machine. His eyes glisten with unshed tears, and I quickly turn to see what has him so upset.

The breath is ripped from me when I see the most beautiful image in the world. I can see everything. The head, his arms, legs... he's beautiful.

I sniffle, unable to look away as Harris begins to point out different parts of the body, although they are clear to see.

I squeeze Mason's hand before turning to him, finding a few tears escaping down his cheeks. "It's our baby," I whisper.

He squeezes my hand tighter and opens his mouth to form words, but nothing comes out. I can understand his emotion. I'm feeling the same thing.

Not wanting to miss another second, I turn back to the screen, not bothering to wipe away the tears as I stare, riveted by my baby. A giggle slips free when I see him move. It feels foreign since I can also feel him move inside of me.

It's all overwhelming.

When he moves again, his hand going to his mouth whilst his leg rests up at a weird angle, I begin to worry.

"Is he safe at that angle?" I ask.

"Perfectly safe in there. You have a healthy baby. In fact, going by these measurements, I'd say you are looking at an eight-pound baby when they're born."

That sounds big.

Then I remember the story I read online, and my eyes bug out. "Measure him again. Eight pounds? Oh my God, I'm going to be torn in two," I cry out, unable to look away from my baby.

Mason doesn't bother to hide his amusement when he lifts my hand up to his lips. "You can do this," he declares.

"Says you, the one who doesn't have to push him out," I reply smartly.

"Would you like to know the sex of the baby?" the doctor asks.

Mason and I exchange a look before turning to Harris and nodding. We discussed this yesterday and came to the decision to find out.

I want to have a boy just like his father, who will have his hair and those gorgeous brown eyes. Mason, however, wants a girl. He grew up in a house full of boys, and to me, that's reason enough. He said he wants a girl with my hair, and my personality. It made me open up to him a little bit more.

As hard as I'm denying this—denying us—I know he meant every word. He wasn't playing games with me.

"Let me see," the doctor murmurs, pressing the wand back onto my stomach. "Ah, there we are. You are having a... girl," he reveals. "Congratulations. I'll print some pictures off here and you can collect and pay for them at the reception desk. I just need to make up your next appointment, so I'll leave you to get cleaned up and I will be back shortly. Do you have any questions before I leave?"

Too lost for words, my eyes transfixed on the screen, I shake my head.

A girl!

We're going to have a girl!

The door shutting startles me, and I turn to Mason with a watery smile, his own expression mirroring mine.

"We're having a girl," he whispers huskily, the emotion raw in his voice.

"Yes, we are," I croak out, my head filled with so much happiness it's overwhelming.

"We're having a girl," he repeats, his eyes still glued to the screen where the last picture Mr. Harris captured of the baby is still showing. He stays like that for a few more seconds, before looking back down at me. "We're having a fucking girl," he shouts, grinning like a fool. I grin back, loving that he's as excited as I am.

"We are," I repeat softly, then watch in amazement as his face softens and tears fall from his eyes. The first one hits his lap before he realises that he's even crying, and when he does, he grabs my face in his rough palms and leans forward. The movement catches me so off guard that I'm not prepared when he leans in and kisses me. It's soft and slow at first, and I will admit, I'm a little hesitant. But when I feel his tongue at the seam of my lips, I give in, kissing him back.

I feel the kiss all the way down to my toes, his touch setting my entire body on fire. I moan into his mouth, my tongue massaging his.

God, he tastes good!

He shifts off the chair, standing to lean over me. One hand cups my cheek still, while the other roams down the side of my body, over my stomach. I gasp at the sharp kick on my bladder from our girl.

"You okay?" he asks, pulling back. "I'm sorry if I've pushed you, but I couldn't let that moment pass without kissing you."

I push him away from me, ignoring the hurt that crosses his features. "I need to piss," I yell, wiping away the gel on my stomach.

Realisation hits, and he quickly helps me off the bed. As much as I'd have loved to keep kissing him, there is no ignoring this.

I hear his laughter when I slam the bathroom door shut, rushing to the toilet to quickly relieve myself.

I drop forward at the relief, smiling to myself. It feels like heaven.

By the time I come out, the doctor is back and talking to Mason near the door.

"So, she has one more scan, then has a check-up with the midwife every so often?" he asks Harris.

"Yes. Her midwife will take regular measurements to make sure the baby is growing nicely and will check the heartbeat at every appointment. Denny will also need more bloodwork taken at the end of next month due to low blood pressure, but it's just a precaution."

"So, everything is okay?"

"Yes," he assures him, then smiles warmly when he notices me. "Feel better?"

"Much. Please tell me I won't need to drink that much again for my next scan?" I ask, not remembering it being this uncomfortable at my first scan. Not that there was a lot to see on my first scan. It just looked like a black blob to me.

"We'll expect you to drink some fluid, but not as much as today."

"Thank God," I breathe out.

"I've written your next appointment down and given the slip to Dad here. If you'd like to collect the pictures at the front desk, they will be ready," he explains.

We both thank him and leave, heading to the reception area to pick up our scan pictures.

"That was incredible," Mason murmurs, staring down at the picture in awe as we make our way back to the car.

"It was. I can't believe we're having a girl," I tell him, feeling warmth hit my chest.

When we get to the car, he helps me back inside.

"Have you decided on names?" Mason asks when he gets in.

"Honestly? No. I don't know why but I hadn't thought that far ahead. I guess a part of me was waiting until you were there to make the decision with me. It still seems surreal that we're having a girl."

"I know what you mean. I'm still trying to process it," he tells me, before going quiet.

When his gaze flicks to me again, I can't help but ask, "What?"

"Thank you. Thank you for letting me share today with you. After everything I've put you through, you could have told me to fuck off and I wouldn't have blamed you," he explains. He clears his throat, turning his attention back to the road. "I could have missed seeing that."

"But you didn't," I tell him, feeling a tightness in my chest at his words. "You were there, and I'm sorry you've already missed so much."

"Let's not dwell on the past. We're here now, together," he tells me, before his smile lights up his entire face. "I'm going to have a daughter. Now I've got two important women to cherish and look after."

Tears fill my eyes at his words. I wish he would stop saying all these things to me because it's making me so damn emotional.

Mason's phone rings, cutting through the silence. He puts it on loudspeaker when he answers.

"So… what are we having? Tell us the news," Max yells through the phone, making me groan.

"No, Max," Mason deadpans.

"Ahhhh, bro, don't be like that. It's not yours, is it? You finally figured it out. But, bro, Denny and I, we have this amazing chemistry—"

"Fuck off, Max," Mason growls, and I let out a giggle. He shoots me a warning glare and I make a motion of zipping my lips, my grin spreading across my face.

"Oh, come on, bro. You wanna be an uncle, I get that, but I'm the daddy—"

"I'm cutting you off, asshole."

"Who's the daddy?" Max sings through the phone. "I'm the mother-fucking daddy."

Mason glares at the phone, and I giggle again, this time ignoring his murderous glare. "Is there something you fucking wanted, Max, other than to piss me off?"

"That's no way to speak to your lover's baby daddy, is it, Mason." When Mason growls, Max wisely stops. "I'm fucking around. Keep ya knickers on. We're all heading over to the Manor. Want to meet us there for lunch and give us the good news?"

"We'll be there," he replies curtly, before adding, "Oh, and Max, I'll be kicking your arse."

When I open my mouth to say something, he gives me a warning look. The smile on my face has my cheeks aching.

W e turn up at the restaurant twenty minutes later with all the gang outside waiting for us. Harlow is the first one to greet us, running into my arms and giving me a tight hug.

"So? What are we expecting—a niece or a nephew?" Maverick calls, the first to ask.

"I'm the daddy, so I should find out first," Max teases, giving me a wink.

My heart melts at their support. More stupid tears fill my eyes as I take in everyone standing around, waiting to be told.

I'm still emotional over Nan's response. She congratulated me and told me having a girl is one of the most precious gifts in this world. I asked what she would have said if it had been a boy, and she snorted and said she would have wished me luck. For me, I know being pregnant is a gift; one I'll cherish forever.

Now that she knows, we don't have any issues with the others knowing.

"We are having a…" I turn to Mason, gesturing for him to finish.

He grins like a kid on Christmas, stepping forward. "We're having a girl," he yells in triumph. He pulls me against his chest, kissing my head as everyone swarms around us to give their congratulations.

It's only when Mark—Mason's granddad—pulls me to the side that things get emotional.

"Girl, you'll never know how pleased I am to see my first great grandbaby coming into the world—and a little girl at that. Apart from their mother, the last female to be born into this family was generations ago," he explains, choked up. "You'll do a fine job of raising that precious baby girl."

I feel for the man. His daughter—Mason's mum—was a coward in my eyes. She never once had her boys' best interests at heart. She ran off, leaving them with an abusive father. I can see the unnecessary guilt consuming Mark, but he isn't to blame for his daughter's sins.

"And you'll be a fantastic granddad," I tell him, sniffling.

"You upsetting my girl, Granddad?" Mason teases, stepping up beside me.

My girl! He called me his girl.

"No, son. Just letting her know how pleased I am that she's a part of this family, and for giving me a granddaughter." He turns to me, his expression adoring. "You picked a fine one, my boy."

"Thank you," I whisper, choked up.

This is all too much. I'm just Denny. Plus, I still haven't decided what to do.

When Mark steps forward and pulls me into his arms, I collapse into them. I breathe him in, his musky, detergent scent reminding me of my granddad when he was alive. It's comforting.

"You're good for him, girl," he whispers into my ear. When he pulls back, his gaze flickers over to where Maverick has pulled Mason to the side. "I know my grandson can be a little hot-headed, but he didn't mean to hurt you. I don't think the others noticed, but I could see it was killing him. I watched him pull further and further away each time he did it. I'm glad you've come back to him."

His words cause the dam inside of me to burst. And they aren't silent tears. They are loud, gut-wrenching sobs.

I throw myself back into his arms. "Thank you for wanting me here," I croak out between sobs.

Warm hands gently pry me away from Mark. I'm turned and pulled into a set of strong arms. I don't need to see who it is. I just know. His scent, his warmth… it cocoons me like a safety net.

"Hey, what's all this about?" he whispers, his breath against my neck. I shiver.

"Nothing. I'm being silly," I tell him, pulling away to wipe under my eyes. "I'm just not used to this." I wave my hand around us, but then I see everyone has left. "Where did they go?"

"Inside to give us some privacy. Now, what has you so upset? Talk to me."

"Honestly, I'm just being stupid."

"Try me," he demands gently.

I sigh, then let it all out. "My family isn't like yours, Mase. They aren't close. Even me and my brother aren't that close. He wasn't happy about the pregnancy, and yeah, he would have helped if I asked. But it's not the same. My nan has been supportive, and I'd never have gotten through the past couple of months without her. Hell, I wouldn't have made it this far in life had it not been for her. But your family… they've done nothing but be happy for me. And they're the ones who have the right to be angry at me." I stop, wiping the snot on the sleeve of my cardigan as more tears flow. "And your granddad… he accepted me. He's happy it's me carrying his grandchild."

"Angel, you are our family now. It isn't just you anymore. You've just taken on another family by agreeing to have our baby. You're not going anywhere, and I promise I'm going to make up for all the shit I put you through to get you to stay where you belong," he swears.

I want to tell him he doesn't need to try, that I'm staying. After seeing his reaction at the scan today, there is no way I can leave. I can't take her away from him. The words form on my lips, but nothing comes out.

My stomach grumbles, and Mason looks down, smiling affectionately at my rounded stomach. "Let's go feed you and our daughter. We can worry about the rest tomorrow, okay? Let's just celebrate the good news."

I nod, taking his offered hand. He's right. We shouldn't be dwelling on the past.

We should be celebrating the news of our baby girl.

CHAPTER
SEVEN

DENNY

My mind is on the court case tomorrow. It had been postponed once again due to new evidence turning up, and I'm anxious as hell.

I have a group of amazing people around me, who will support me on the day, but I really need my brother. He promised me he would be here, and he isn't.

I have been here at his place for three weeks, hoping he would be back. He isn't calling or messaging me back either, but he has been in communication with Lexi. A few days after her outburst, she came to me and said she had spoken to him. Apparently, he's okay.

I don't get it. What work does he do that causes him to be away from the phone every day? And why can't he pick up the phone for his own sister?

I need to hear his voice, to listen to him telling me that it will all be okay. I'm scared about getting on that stand in front of all those people.

Mason promised to be with me every step of the way, and I'm grateful. He has been patient with me since the scan, giving me my space to process everything and come to a decision. I just need to get that tiny worm of doubt out of my head that's telling me he won't want this long-term.

And tonight, he's going to take me out to take my mind off it. But I can't for the life of me find something to wear.

"Denny," Harlow calls. "I'm here."

"I'm back here," I call out, grateful she's here. "I have nothing to wear. Most of these are before Bump. I'll never get them over my boobs or hips."

"Are you still stressing?" she asks, walking into the room with some bags.

"Yes. All of them are skin-tight and I don't know why I packed them. I'm not even going to attempt to try one because I'm scared it will squish baby girl."

"You're such a drama queen," she teases, before holding up one of the bags. "Now, don't get mad, but I bought you a present. You were always there for me, lending me clothes to impress Malik, so I thought I'd return the favour."

I take the beautiful green halter maxi-dress from the bag, in love with the diamond stud in the centre. The material at the back is longer, reaching the floor, but the front I reckon with my bump, will fall above my knees.

"Harlow," I muse, holding it.

She presses her hands together. "Tell me you like it"

"I love it," I admit, knowing this is something I would have picked out for myself. "Thank you so much."

"Yay! I saw it and immediately thought of you. I think all your shopping torture rubbed off on me," she teases, reminding me of our shopping excursion to find her some lingerie to seduce Malik in.

I laugh, wanting to reveal I went easy that day. "Thank you."

"Is it okay if I wait for Malik to pick me up? He's passing by soon with Maverick and offered to pick me up. He shouldn't be long."

"Yeah, you can tell me why you had to end the call so quickly this morning," I press.

She blows out a breath. "Don't ask."

"What's wrong?" I ask, sitting up.

"Aunt Flow came to visit this morning," she groans.

Ahh. "That's one thing I've not missed."

She narrows her gaze on me. "It's not even the worst part. Grams used it as an excuse to have the sex talk with me again. Since you got pregnant, she's been worried we aren't using protection."

"But I did," I point out. I wasn't on the pill either, since my mum refused to let me take it. She thought giving it to me was like giving me permission to whore myself out. "I think he just had super sperm."

"Well, Grams told Malik to take one of Mark's condoms and not take any risks," she reveals, then mimicking her gram's voice, she says, "I'm too young to be a great grammy."

I snort as I strip out of my clothes to try on the dress. It fits like a glove. "Why are they using condoms?"

She makes air quotes. "It spices things up in the bedroom."

"Your nan is fucking nuts," I muse, chortling. "What did Malik do?"

"Left me to listen to the rest of the lecture," she admits, frowning when her phone goes off with a message. "Malik is on his way."

"Are you nervous about tomorrow?" I ask. I've not admitted it out loud, but the fact they've not been able to locate Hannah is worrying me.

"A little bit," she reveals, letting out a sigh. "I'm worried what Hannah's disappearance means. Her mum is adamant that she never ran away, and she thinks something has happened to Hannah."

"Everything will be fine. I'm sure of it," I assure her, gripping her shoulder in a firm squeeze. "We have enough evidence to back up our story. He's going to go down."

"I guess," she whispers.

Seeing she has more to say, I sit down on the bed next to her. "What's on your mind?"

She runs her fingers through her hair. "Don't get me wrong, I know what she did was unforgivable; but what if she hasn't run away? We're all bad-mouthing her when something serious could have happened to her."

"That bloody jacket could mean anything. She may have planted it there."

"Maybe. It just doesn't sit right with me. I've been trying to tell Malik this, but he doesn't want to hear it. He doesn't care. In his eyes, if something's happened to her, she deserves it. I just feel it in my gut that something bad has happened."

I can understand Malik's feelings over the matter. I hate Hannah, but… she's still human. She doesn't deserve to be hurt.

"I hate Hannah for what she put you through, so I can relate with Malik. If she is hurt, then that isn't your fault. She made her bed, Harlow. Stop letting her get to you. She isn't even here and she's doing it."

She groans, falling onto her back. "I know. It's probably nerves, what with the case starting."

"Probably."

Her phone rings and she lifts her head to see the screen. "Malik is outside, but if you want, I can stay and help you get ready."

"No, I've got this."

She sits up and presses a kiss to my cheek. "Call me if you need me."

I nod and watch her leave before stepping back out of my dress to go and take a shower. It takes me longer than I planned for to get ready, but once I am done, I glance in the bedroom mirror one last time.

I feel sexy for the first time in months. My cleavage is pushed up and together and the dress clings to my bump in just the right way. I'm glad I brought my dangly silver earrings and necklace because it fits snugly between my breasts.

I kept my makeup light, and left my hair to dry naturally, not having the energy to do more.

I fluff it once more, trying to get some oomph, when there's a knock on the door.

I rush down the hall, fighting the urge to chew on my nails. "Coming," I call out.

Mason greets me on the other side when I pull open the door. His gaze immediately drops to my cleavage. His eyes darken, and pleasure rolls over me.

When his gaze hits my stomach, a soft smile tugs at his lips. He has an unhealthy obsession with my pregnancy.

I can't hide my reaction. Desire pools between my legs, and I sway slightly against the door.

I want him.

I want him so goddamn much it hurts.

I squeeze my thighs together, trying to ease the ache pulsing between my legs. His lips pull into his signature smirk when he notices my reaction. It's the same smirk that got me crushing on him five years ago at fourteen years old. Even back then, I knew the guy behind the smirk had the power to get me to do whatever he wanted. And I didn't care.

If I could go back and give my fourteen-year-old self a slap, I would. I'd tell her she would grow feelings for him.

Because trust me, I have.

"You look... Fuck! You look beautiful, Denny," he tells me, his voice hoarse.

My cheeks heat at his appraisal, and I do my own appreciative scan of his attire. "Thank you. You don't look too bad yourself."

I'm lying. He looks freaking hot. I've never seen Mason dressed up like this before, not the full kit anyway. He even has his black leather shoes on. His dark purple shirt is unbuttoned at the top of his chest. The sleeves are rolled up to his elbows, giving me a clear view of the muscles in his arms and the veins that pulse up the inside of them.

He's wearing his favourite jeans, the ones that aren't ripped or stained. They showcase his thick, muscular thighs. They aren't built like tree trunks, but they are powerful all the same.

All the Carter's ooze confidence, some more than others, but Mason wears his in a subtle way.

It's such a turn on.

And since I have his delicious body burned into my memory, it's torture to keep my hands to myself.

Shaking away my thoughts before I end up turning into a wanton hussy and jumping him, I give him a bright smile and take a step towards him.

"You look *really* good," I let out, exhaling heavily.

My stomach rumbles, and his lips twitch in amusement. "Let's go before you decide to eat me."

Don't tempt me.

He takes my hand, helping me out of the door, and I have to hold back a shiver.

This is going to be a long night.

———

Mason and I are seated straight away thanks to him pre-booking the table. The quirky little restaurant is thirty minutes away from home, and a place I have never eaten at before. After scanning the décor, I'm surprised I haven't. It's a place my mother would rejoice in, with its antique décor, candlelight setting and famous literature lining the shelves near the entrance. The blood-red walls match nicely with the dark wooden furniture and mahogany beams.

Even with all the quirky and expensive furnishings, it still manages to be inviting with its homey feel. And the different aromas in the air are making me hungry.

The reason I know my mother hasn't been here is because of the outside. It doesn't look like much and isn't in the nicest of places, which was kind of foolish of the owners. I'm surprised this place hasn't been robbed.

The outside has cracked, chipped paint. When we were walking up from the car park, I expected to be taken to a shit hole.

Mason watches me closely as we take our seats. "I know the outside doesn't look like much, but I can promise you, the food is great."

Reaching over, I pat his hand. "Stop worrying. I like it. It's different."

He sags against his chair. "Thank God. I used to come here with my nan. She loved it. I haven't been here since she died. It didn't feel the same."

"But—" I begin, worried I'm tarnishing a memory.

"As soon as you agreed to come with me, I knew this was the perfect place to come."

I wipe my sweaty palms down my thighs. I love that he brought me to a place that holds meaning to him. It makes this entire night more special. "Thank you. I'm glad that you did."

The corner of his lips tips up in a half smile. "Their menu is mostly Italian, but I know Nick will make you whatever you like, babe."

"I'm not fussy," I assure him, then lean forward, wanting to start a conversation. "What was your nan like?"

I don't remember much about their nan. She died not long after they moved here. My nan—from my mum's side, who volunteers at the school—knew her. They went to the same church, so I got to meet her a few times.

"She was amazing. She wasn't our biological nan, but it didn't stop us from treating her and loving her as one. I wish we'd had more time with her. It's been hard since she died."

"She died not long after you moved in with your granddad, right?"

"Yeah. Six months after. We might not have had much time with her, but she taught us a lot. She taught us it was okay to be sensitive, whereas Granddad taught us to be men. When she gave you her attention, you had all of it. She never let us feel like we were a hindrance or getting in the way. She was so full of life."

"She sounds amazing."

"She really was. If she was here right now, she'd kick my arse to Belgium and back. She had so much fight in her for someone who was only four-foot-nine." He pauses, chuckling. "She had Granddad wrapped around her finger. They were best friends. But if he pissed her off, he'd be toast."

I lean in closer, loving this side of him. When he speaks about her, he looks carefree, and his features turn child-like somewhat.

"What about your other nan?"

His lips twist, and instantly, I regret asking. "She died, but she and

Granddad were over before that. She left him before our mum was born and never reached out again. It wasn't until Mum had us and moved back here needing money, that Granddad finally got to meet her."

I pale, hating how close it came to that being us. "Just like I did."

No wonder his granddad was so emotional about me coming back. His story ended differently to ours.

"No. You are nothing like that, Denny."

"I'm sorry," I tell him, letting out a breath.

"What about your nan, the one from Wales?"

Thankful he's steered the conversation away, I answer, "Well, she *will* be kicking your arse when she sees you," I tell him, keeping my face straight. When he pales, I begin to laugh. "I'm kidding. *Kind of.* She's cool, and nothing like my dad. She's opinionated, strong, worldly, funny, youthful, and totally loveable. And my biggest supporter. She does have a house here, but she prefers the solitude of Wales."

"What about your other nan? Didn't your nan work at the school?" he asks, making me groan.

"Yeah. We used to get along, until the night I kicked you in the balls," I tell him, my voice trailing off. I really shouldn't have reminded him of that. I wince just thinking about it, remembering the sound of his pain.

But he did deserve it.

Harlow and I had gone to a party after one of Malik's races and Mason turned up with some girl all over him. When he started spouting crap at me, I lost it and kneed him in the balls.

Not one of my finest moments.

He grimaces, shifting in his seat. "I remember."

I chuckle when his hand reaches under the table, no doubt checking his balls. I shouldn't find it amusing. What I did to him was stupid and dangerous, but totally justified.

"Anyway, after that, I got completely wasted. I think one of Nan's friends saw me walking home and reported back. My nan told Mum, and all hell broke loose. Until then, I think my nan trusted my judgement and behaviour. She used to say Mum was too hard on me and that I was a sharp, clever girl who had her head on straight."

"And now?"

I shrug, reaching for the glass of water the waitress leaves. "She's religious, so she told me I shamed her and their family and I shouldn't speak to her until I got God's forgiveness. Since I'm not going to be meeting the big guy any time soon, she's gonna have to wait," I joke, hoping to lighten the conversation.

Mason frowns. "But it's upset you."

"Not really. I guess I knew who my nan truly was. She's kind of a mirror person of my mum, but her nice act isn't fake. She's lovely to everyone. Though admittedly, she's stubborn and set in her ways. I answered back for the first time that day and made it worse, so she might not have reacted as badly as she did, but it's not the point." I grimace when I think of the things they said to me. "Can I ask you something?"

"Anything," he agrees, just as the waitress arrives to take our order.

"You can order for me," I tell him, and he nods, listing off foods that have me licking my lips.

When he's done, he leans back in his chair, appraising me. "What did you want to ask me?"

My hands shake a little. I hope I'm not making a mistake in bringing this up. I just want to get to know him. "What was your dad like? I remember you said you were scared about us being together because of him. Can you tell me why? I know some, but it's not something Harlow and I like to gossip about. We respect people's privacy. My nan heard stuff and repeated it to me that day, and the rest I kind of pieced together and Harlow confirmed it."

He places his drink down, sinking back into his chair. "I…" He pauses, running a hand through his hair.

I'm such an idiot. It's no secret that their relationship wasn't good, and my need to understand him more has just upset him.

I place my hand over his. "It's okay. I shouldn't have asked. You can tell me about your job instead," I tell him, keeping my voice light.

He watches me for a moment, colour returning to his cheeks.

"Sorry, it's just hard to talk about," he admits. "But if we're going to be together, it's only fair you know everything. I just don't know how much I can tell you. I can tell you about what I went through, but not the rest. My brothers' stories are not mine to tell."

"You don't need to tell me," I declare, when he begins to tap his fingers relentlessly on the table. "I don't want our date to be ruined by talking about something that upsets you."

The flash of pain and vulnerability in his eyes when he looks up from the table takes me off guard. I've never seen it before, not when he hides behind his charm and easy-going behaviour.

"It's not going to ruin the date. We're here to get to know each other better," he explains, before taking my hand. "Maybe if I can get you to understand my past, you'll understand somewhat as to why I did what I did with you."

He isn't comfortable sharing this, and I hate that he's only doing it to make me happy. "Why don't you just tell me what you're comfortable with?"

He nods and takes a swig of his Coke before starting. "I need you to promise me something first."

"What?" I ask.

"Don't leave. If you don't want to try at a relationship because of what I did, I'll hate it, but I'll understand; but please don't leave me because of what I'm about to tell you. Or look at me different."

Now I'm worried. "I swear to you."

He clears his throat. "As you know, my dad was violent. From as far back as I can remember, he laid into us. Malik and Maverick had it bad. They were beaten to the point they couldn't go to school some days. But me… me, he…" He swallows, ducking his head.

I grab his hand as a lump forms in my throat. I hate his dad. I hate that I brought this up. "What about you?" I whisper.

"He didn't just beat me," he croaks out, meeting my gaze now, as if he had to inwardly prepare himself to say it. "He would drag me out of bed during the night. First, he would beat me, make sure I couldn't fight back or move much, but then he would take me down into the cellar."

My breath catches in my throat, and unshed tears burn my eyes. I hate that this happened to him. "Mason, you don't need to say anything more."

"I do," he tells me, waiting for a waitress to pass by before continuing. "No one else knows, or at least, I don't think they do. I've never wanted to talk about it, and I think they knew that."

"Did he…" I clear my throat, unable to finish the sentence.

"No," he admits, his jaw clenched. "He'd have women down there waiting to have sex with me. It was humiliating. They'd laugh at my inexperience, and taunt me. They didn't care if they were hurting me." He pauses, taking another swig of his drink. I feel sick, dizzy. I can't imagine what that did to him; how he could bear another woman's touch after what he went through. "Something inside me snapped when I turned thirteen. I wanted to prove something to myself, I guess. It's the reason I slept around. I wanted the choice," he explains, trailing off.

I cover my mouth with my hand. "Mason, I'm so sorry," I blubber.

"Don't cry for me," he pleads hoarsely. "It's over."

I can't help it. I can hear the torment and pain in his voice, and it's tearing me in two. His dad was a monster. I can understand his reasons for sleeping around. It was about taking his power back.

"How old were you when it all started?"

"Eight, nine—I'm not sure. It all blurs together," he tells me, unable to meet my gaze. I squeeze his hand, waiting until he looks at me to answer.

"I'm so sorry, Mason."

"Now can you see why I was trying to protect you? I have his DNA coursing through my blood, Denny. It's evil. I couldn't taint you with that, not when I felt what I did for you. It scares me. It was never meant to be more. I woke up and saw the bedsheets and I broke. I took the one thing from you that you could never get back, just like my dad. I had turned out just like him, and I hated myself."

I shake my head, denying his words. "You're nothing like him, Mason. I'm not going to lie and say I only wanted that night. I did want more. But it doesn't change what we shared. I chose to lose my virginity to you that night, and I don't regret it. No matter what happened between us after, it still meant everything to me that it was you. I chose you, Mason. I *chose* you."

"And I ruined it," he murmurs, running a hand over his face.

I wipe under my eyes, hoping like hell my mascara is actually waterproof like it said it was. "What changed your mind about me the day I left? I don't understand how you went from one extreme to another."

"I was tired of wanting you and not having you. It was selfish of me, but the minute Harlow told me you were leaving, it was like something snapped inside me. It was then that I knew I would never hurt you, and that I couldn't let you go. She had barely explained what was happening before I started to chase after you. When you left, it was like a part of me left with you." He takes a breath, his gaze burning into mine. "Then she told me you were pregnant, and I knew… I knew I'd rather have my limbs torn off than see either of you hurt by me or anyone else."

I'm struck hard by his words, the breath whooshing out of me. It was real. All of it. He isn't saying this to get what he wants; he's telling me to make me understand. This isn't a game to him. It isn't an obligation.

"What about your mum? Didn't she try to take you away from him?" I ask, unsure what to say to his previous declaration.

Although I knew parts about his dad, it was his mum no one ever really spoke about. All Malik told Harlow was that she left them as kids and never came back.

Mason's laughter is forced. "My mum was worse than my dad in a way. Maverick painted her out to be a saint to us all, but I know better. I think he was protecting Malik and the twins, I'm not sure. But I remember. It's something I can't get into. It's Maverick's story."

"Has she ever tried to see you?"

"No, thank God," he bursts out. "She didn't want us, angel. She wanted the benefits she got so she could feed her drug habit. Granddad said she was a really good mother when we were first born, and I take his word for it, but again, I think he just wants us to have something nice to remember instead of the nightmare we lived.

"The mother I knew was always shitfaced, high off whatever drug she could afford, or passed out somewhere. I can't even tell you how many times we walked in on her fucking one or more of Dad's mates. Dad was either fucking some other chick or passed out next to them. Neither of them raised us. Maverick did. From the age of five, he was cooking us meals with whatever scraps he could find in the cupboard. Not them."

I can't imagine what that was like as a child. My parents seem like angels compared to his.

"I'm sorry, Mason. For all of it. You should never have gone through that."

"Some people shouldn't have kids," he tells me, shrugging.

I force out a laugh. "I can relate there. There are couples out there who deserve to have a child, who will give it a good home, love, and raise them with pride. I've never understood my mum, but since being pregnant, it's worse. I thought maybe it was something I did, but I'm realising now, it's them who are the problem. Not me. Because I couldn't even imagine not being able to love our baby."

"You're going to be a great mum," he assures me.

"I'm going to try."

"I don't think you'll have to. I think it will come naturally," he tells me, smiling at me.

I sigh, squeezing his hand. "And you're going to be a great father. Don't doubt that."

"I promise I'll be the best father to our daughter, the best man to you. I'll never do anything to hurt either of you."

"I know you won't, Mason. The thought never even entered my mind. You're nothing like your parents. You're loyal, honourable, and courageous. You're charming, loving, and funny. But most of all, you're protective. You could have a gun pointed to your head and you'd still never hurt us."

His eyes glisten with tears and his mouth opens, then closes. He sags against the table. "You really think that?" he asks, his voice choked up.

"I do. Without a doubt," I assure him. "You take care of those closest to you. When you laugh, people laugh with you. If you hurt, people hurt with you. Your moods spread like wildfire, but when you care, you make everyone feel safe. We know nothing can stand in your way of helping those around you."

I tilt my chin down when he continues to stare at me. I hadn't meant to be that honest. But once I started, it kept flowing and I couldn't stop. Plus, he needs to know what he means to those around him.

I'm grateful when the waitress arrives with our food, breaking the silence. She sets our food down on the table before walking off.

The minute the intoxicating scent reaches my senses, I pick up the fork and dive into the rich-smelling spaghetti.

As far as first dates go, this one has to be one of the best. Not that I have anything to compare it to.

It's nice getting to know him, despite how the conversation turned. But I can see he's trying. I can see this is the beginning of something new.

I didn't want to get my hopes up, but it's already too late.

How could they not?

It's Mason.

CHAPTER
EIGHT

DENNY

I reach out, trying to turn off the dreadful noise coming from the alarm on my phone. I groan when it slips off the bedside table and falls to the floor, where it continues to blare. I'm not ready to get up. It feels like it was only five minutes ago that I got into bed. I know that isn't the case. It's because I didn't get in until gone half eleven last night, and since I got pregnant, I haven't been awake after nine. My body isn't used to it.

With a yawn, I roll onto my side and grab my phone from the floor. I switch off the alarm before deciding to scroll through Facebook. If there's one thing that can wake me up, it's nosing at other people's posts.

A grin tugs at my lips when I see twenty-six notifications, but as soon as I click on them, my grin slips. They're all group invitations or a notification to tell me someone I wasn't even friends with posted in 'said' group.

Whatever.

Clicking on my newsfeed, I'm even more disappointed. There isn't even a cute picture of a kitten or a funny meme. It's filled with people moaning about their lives.

I hate this side of social media. Not all the time though. There are times when I do click on comments just to read them. And I bet I'm not the only one there for the comments.

My favourites are the hypocritical, cryptic ones. Like the one a girl from my old school has written.

If you're going to write a status about me, at least tag me in it, you bitch. Or better yet, stop hiding behind your computer and say it to my face.

I desperately want to comment and say, 'Why haven't you tagged the person?', but I can't. I don't get involved in other people's drama.

The rest of my newsfeed is the same, some going on about being the 'bigger person'.

Dropping the phone to the bed, I let out a sigh. I need to get up anyway if I want to be ready in time to meet up with the others.

Sliding out of the bed, a wave of dizziness hits me, and the room begins to blur. I sit back down on the edge, tilting my head down as I wait for the nausea to subside.

"Please don't be sick. Please don't be sick," I chant, taking deep breaths. It's something my nan told me to do when I first started getting morning sickness.

When my phone beeps with an incoming message, I ignore the dizziness and reach for it. I chuckle when I see what Mason put his name under.

I'm the daddy: *Do you want me to pick you up to go for some break-fast? Harlow and Malik said they'll come with us as her lawyer called to tell us it's been postponed for another hour. M x*

I didn't even realise he put his name under that last night because I had been too tired to even look. I should have known though. Max had been teasing him relentlessly about who the daddy was.

Denny: *That sounds awesome. I'll jump in the shower now. I'm dying for a cup of tea, but I don't think we have any milk. D x*

I'm the daddy: *That's not a visual I need right now when I'm having* *a coffee with Granddad and Joan. That woman can smell a boner a mile off. M x*

I chuckle at the visual. I wouldn't put it past Joan. She's like a horny granny on Viagra.

I can't stop the sly smirk when I begin to type out my reply.

Denny: Phew. I'm glad I didn't tell you I was already naked and just about to get into the shower. That would have been soooo awkward. ;) D x

This is what it was like between us before we slept together. It was easy banter and flirting. I've missed it. Missed him. There's no denying it, especially after last night when he revealed his past to me. It feels like I got to know him on a deeper level than the façade he puts on for those around him.

I'm the daddy: *Shit! Things just got really awkward in the kitchen. Think of me, angel, when you're in the shower, all hot, wet, soapy... yeah, I need to stop. See you soon, gorgeous. M x*

Harlow: Are you texting Mason? Because he just went fifty shades of red and spilt my bloody orange juice all over the table.

Chuckling, I reply to Harlow first with a winky emoji, before replying to Mason.

Denny: I guess... I mean, I'll be all wet, slick... I'll have to picture something.

I'm the daddy: You're mean, Denny Smith. Get your cute arse in that shower. Be there in twenty. M x

Denny: Promises, promises ;)

I'm the daddy: *Now I need a shower. M x*

My cheeks ache from smiling as I throw my phone down onto the bed. When I turn to grab my stuff, my court outfit catches my eye, and I frown.

When I bought it, I was a lot smaller. Over the past three weeks, I've grown rapidly. Now, I'm worried it isn't going to fit me in the same way, even though the black, sleek dress is stretchy. I want them to take me seriously and they won't if I arrive looking like I can't dress properly.

I love it though, which is why I brought it with me. Nan even said that from behind, you can't tell I'm pregnant, until I turn and you see my bump.

With that thought in mind, I quickly race through my morning routine, wanting to be dressed before the others get here.

I'm just adding the finishing touches to my makeup when there's a knock at the front door. Grabbing my bag off the bed, I walk to the front room, throwing the bag over my shoulder.

"Hey," I greet when I pull open the door.

Mason's gaze runs over my body, lingering again on my obscene cleavage. I was right;, the dress doesn't fit like it did before, but it's the only thing I have in a dull colour. Everything else is bright and summery.

I desperately want to rearrange the cups of the dress, so my boobs aren't so much on show. It's getting uncomfortable having them pushed together.

I arch an eyebrow at Mason. "Are you finished?"

His smirk has my stomach fluttering and my knees locking together. The hold he has over my body scares me sometimes. It's like I have no power or will when it comes to him.

"Give me a sec," he replies, rolling his gaze over me once more.

I shove him backwards, causing him to laugh. "Stop!"

"Oi! Once you've finished ogling the hot MILF, can we get going?" Max yells. I look beyond Mason to see him hanging out of the car window, grinning from ear to ear.

"Bro," Mason growls, slowly turning to face his brother. I lock up, following him down the path.

When we get close, Max takes his teasing one step further and his eyes begin to gleam. Slowly, he shows his appreciation, licking his lips as he eyes me up and down.

"You're dead," Mason growls, but Max wisely shuts the window, blocking Mason from getting to him.

Mason shakes his head, muttering under his breath as he opens the passenger side door. With one leg in, he puts his hand over mine, stopping me. I meet his gaze, and he whispers, "You look seriously fucking hot today, by the way."

My cheeks heat. I love that he still finds me attractive with the massive bump. "Thank you."

"No need to thank me. I'll always tell you the truth," he admits, before a devilish smirk reaches his lips. "You should know: you remind me of a naughty, hot school teacher right now, and I'm having dirty thoughts."

"I—"

"Come on, we haven't got all day," Max yells from inside the car.

Mason growls as I chuckle, sliding into the car. I'm stunned by his comment, flattered in a way, but he really needs to stop making me so hot and bothered around him.

He shuts the door behind me before walking around the car. I turn slightly to Max. "Stop teasing him."

"I can't help it," he admits, chuckling. When Mason gets into the car as I'm buckling my seatbelt, Max exhales dramatically. "Denny, you're gonna kill me, love."

"Huh?" I mutter, shoving my bag to the floor by my feet.

"I had a semi hard-on before you got in the car, but now I've got a raging boner from looking at your tits. The seatbelt has made them—"

"Stop looking at my…"

I trail off, my eyebrows bunching together when Mason unclips his belt and gets out of the car.

Shit.

He opens the backdoor and drags Max out onto the ground. Max, unfazed, lets Mason lift him to his feet.

"Talk to my girl like that again, Max, and I swear to God, I'll do more than kick your arse. I'll make you shit teeth."

Max holds up his hands, still grinning. "Kinky. I hope you don't talk to Denny with that mouth."

"Max, I swear to fucking God, I'll tell everyone you have an STD so you never get laid again."

Max's grin slips. "You wouldn't."

"Try me," Mason warns, letting him go. "Now, apologise."

His girl!

He called me his girl. I like how it sounds.

I wait silently until they're both back in the car. "Um…"

"Don't apologise for his behaviour. I'm fine," Max tells me, but tenses when Mason growls low in his throat. "I'm sorry I spoke to you like that, Den."

"It's okay," I assure him, turning to face the front window.

I smile to myself, Mason's words going through my mind.

"What are you so happy about?" Mason asks, looking at me warily, before quickly looking up in the rear-view mirror to check on Max. Probably to make sure he isn't doing anything.

Not willing to tell him the truth as he pulls off, I say, "Nothing."

————

W e arrive at the cafe at the same time Harlow, Myles and Malik arrive.

When I see how pale Harlow looks, I step up to her. "Hey, how are you doing?"

I know she's petrified of seeing Davis again, and I can't blame her. It's unfair that she has to.

"Okay. Just nervous, I guess. He's going to be so close. What if he attacks me?" she whispers, her bottom lip trembling.

Malik steps away from the others, leaving them to go inside whilst coming to her side. "What's going on?"

"Nothing," Harlow replies, pleading with me to keep quiet.

I can't. She needs to tell him her fears. "She's worried about Davis being in the courtroom."

Malik growls and pulls her into his arms. "I knew there was something you weren't telling me."

"I didn't want you to worry," she admits, sniffling into his shirt.

"I'll always worry about you. Is it because you're scared to see him again, because I'll be there, Harlow. I'll never leave you."

"What if he tries to hurt me again? He's going to be so close."

I shiver at the anger radiating off him. "He won't. I promise. I'll kill him if he tries to. But, babe, they have protocols in place to prevent all of that."

She runs a hand over her face. "I'm going to mess up. I know it. I won't be able to answer the questions with him watching me."

Malik smirks down at her. "Then stare at me. I'll make sure your focus is on me, baby," he tells her, winking.

"You can't do that in a courtroom," she whisper-yells, making Malik and I chuckle.

"I'll do what the fuck I like, babe," he tells her fiercely. "Why don't we go get something to eat. Settle your nerves?"

Shit!

It just hit me that I didn't get to stop off at a cashpoint. Although the café isn't horrible, it doesn't look updated either, so I can't see a place like this taking cards.

When we walk in, I glance at the old as shit till and groan.

"Any chance the cafe isn't as old as it looks, and it takes cards?"

"I don't think so," Malik answers, his focus on Harlow's arse as she finds us a table.

"I'm just going to pop down the road to the cashpoint. There's one outside Tesco," I rush out, bumping into a hard chest.

"I don't bloody think so, woman. Go sit your arse down. I've already ordered for you," Mason tells me.

My eyes bug out of their sockets at his tone. "Excuse me?"

"Yeah, *excuse you*. Did you really think I'd let you pay for your own breakfast?"

"Mason, you didn't exactly mention anything to me or even ask me what I wanted to eat. I'm not a fucking mind reader."

"And that's my cue to leave," Malik mumbles, walking off to the counter.

"I shouldn't have to," Mason replies, completely ignoring Malik. "You're my woman and I asked you to come. Now let's go sit down. I've ordered you a large tea and a full English breakfast. I made sure they wouldn't put anything you aren't allowed on there."

When he turns and leaves, I stay glued to the floor, trying to process what happened. Was that an argument? If so, who won?

And why does it feel like he spoke to me like an owner would treat their dog?

"I'm not a fucking dog," I snap, and he pauses, turning to face me. "I'm not going to heel because you said sit."

"I didn't treat you like a fucking dog, Denny," he groans, running his fingers through his dark hair. His muscles bulge as he does it, and my mouth waters, despite my blood pressure rising.

The tension in the room changes. It's no longer anger simmering in the air but desire. He arches an eyebrow as he throws my earlier question back at me. "You finished?"

Jerking out of my daze, a sly grin tugs at my lips, and I step forward, leaning up on my toes. My lips brush his ear as I say, "No, there are far too many clothes in the way for me to finish."

When I pull back, he grips my hip, the touch burning through the material of my dress and sending tingles over my skin. I sway a little, and he steadies me, placing his other hand on my waist.

I hadn't meant for it to come out so dirty, so husky, but it did, and now desire is pooling between my legs.

"You shouldn't play games you can't finish," Mason rumbles, his lips brushing across my jaw.

My chest rises and falls with each deep breath as he continues to stare me down, his eyes hooded.

"I wouldn't bother, Denny. He always wins at staring competitions," Max hollers from his place at the table.

I don't know if he broke the tension between us on purpose to get back at his brother or not, but I'm grateful. I need space between us.

When I reach our table, there's a man blocking the path, his chair pushed out leaving hardly any room to get through. He briefly meets my gaze before going back to his food. The woman on the other table tries to push her chair further in, but she's already pushed up to the table.

Huffing out a breath, I force myself to squeeze past the seat, my stomach brushing the back of the man's back. Mason sidles up beside me and pushes the man's chair in.

"Thanks." I smile, ignoring the man when he protests.

He could see I needed to get through, so it's his own fault. When I turn in his direction, he's glaring, his face red and his moustache covered in beans or tomato sauce. It could be both.

I move to our table, inwardly groaning when I see the only chairs left are next to each other, meaning Mason and I are going to be close once again.

He bends down, whispering against my ear, "Don't think you won't be paying for that little tease back there."

I blush and quickly pull the chair out to take a seat. He chortles when I purposely ignore him, a pout on my face. Myles grins, letting out a laugh when he notices my expression. I glare, silently telling him to 'shut it', which only makes him laugh.

Luckily, the food arrives before Mason can unnerve me any more. I dig in, my stomach grumbling in hunger, when suddenly, my stomach begins to tighten. I push my plate away and grab my tea.

"You not hungry?"

"I was. I didn't feel right when I woke up this morning so it's probably more morning sickness."

"Why didn't you say anything?" he asks, just as the egg falls from Max's fork, splattering against his plate with a wet sound.

I push back my chair, covering my mouth with a hand as I rush for the toilets in the far corner.

Oh God, I'm not going to make it.

Trust us to be sitting the farthest away!

I push through the door, causing it to slam against the wall, before I'm rushing to the toilet and throwing up all my breakfast. A whimper slips through my lips when my bare knees touch the floor and my fingers grip the side of the toilet.

It's one thing to use a public toilet to pee, but it's another to kneel in front of one and get up close and personal.

It's making my stomach turn even more.

I vomit again, praying for this to be over quickly.

The door behind me opens, and from a quick glance, I notice Harlow's shoes. "Shit, are you okay?"

I can't answer. I retch once again, more coming up.

Gross!

What sounds like a scuffle soon turns into arguing on the other side of the door. I hope to God it's not Mason trying to get in, or worse, other customers complaining. I'm pretty sure the shop next door can hear me throwing up, so I hate to think what they can hear. I hope I'm not putting people off their food. It isn't like this place is cheap either, so I hate to think they wasted their money.

"Fuck off!" Mason snaps.

Harlow grimaces. "I'll go out and calm it down out there."

I give her a short nod, closing my eyes as a wave of dizziness hits me. A moment later, I hear the door open again.

"Denny, what can I do?" Mason asks worriedly.

I cringe and wave my arm, pointing to the door. I don't want him to see me like this. Not ever.

When he doesn't leave, I groan and rest my head in my hands, elbows leaning against the dingy toilet, trying to give myself some privacy.

"Should I call an ambulance?" he asks, pacing. "What can I do?"

I blindly reach for the tissue, cringing when I feel it's the cheap paper they used to use in school. I wince at how rough it feels against my skin as I wipe my mouth. Reluctantly, I get to my feet, deflating when I see his downturned expression.

He pulls me into his arms, hugging the life out of me, and I have to catch my breath.

"Oxygen is becoming an issue here, Mason," I wheeze, hoping I don't vomit again.

"Are you okay?" he asks, running his gaze over me like I'm injured and not vomiting into a toilet.

I step back so he doesn't smell the vomit on my breath. "I'm fine. It's normal to get sickness during pregnancy. I had it a lot when I moved in with Nan, and a little before, but I haven't had it since," I explain, shrugging. I step to the side so I can reach the sink, gagging at the sight of the dirty, rusty stainless steel.

Sensing my dilemma, Mason hands me a water bottle, and I sigh with relief. "Thank you."

"I asked Myles to get it for you when I heard you being sick. They wouldn't let me in," he explains, rubbing the back of his neck. "I didn't think you'd want to drink the tap water in here." He looks down at the sink, grimacing. "I'm glad they sold it in bottles."

I smile at his thoughtfulness and kindness. "I appreciate it," I croak out.

Turning away from him, I take a large gulp, swirling the water around my mouth before spitting it into the sink. I already feel better, although the taste of vomit still lingers.

When the cool water feels good on my throat, I begin to down it.

"Maybe you should have sipped that," he warns.

I yawn, feeling like I could easily go back to sleep. "It's fine."

He doesn't look convinced. "I'm going to talk to the lawyer about postponing your testimony. Why don't you go sit in the car until I get back."

"What? Why?" I ask.

"Because you're sick," he points out.

"I'm fine. Plus, I've got to be there in… Shit! I have to be there in ten minutes," I squeak, rushing towards the door, but a large arm goes around my waist, under my boobs, pulling me back.

"You can't stand up in court when you look like you're about to pass out, Denny. You need to go home and rest."

"I'm bloody doing no such thing, you idiot. I'm going. I was just sick, which is normal during pregnancy, Mason. I'll go home to sleep after. Don't make me use your brothers against you," I warn, which causes his lips to twitch.

"I don't like this," he protests, before pulling the bathroom door open, revealing everyone standing there, looking concerned. "Before any of you say anything, I tried to talk her out of going."

My gaze lands on Max, and I rear back when I see the bruise already swelling around his eye. "Oh my god. What happened to your eye?"

He ducks his head, pouting. "Nothing. Just walked into a door," he whispers, flinching when I take a step forward.

Malik, Myles and Mason all look at him, open-mouthed. I take another step, glaring at the others when he whimpers. Harlow giggles from the left of me, and I give her the same glare.

"It's not funny. Who hurt you, Max?" I urge, wondering why his brothers haven't kicked their arses.

His eyes widen, filled with fear as they dart behind me. "It was Mason," he whispers, a squeak escaping him when Mason growls and steps forward.

I stop him from going after Max, jabbing him in the chest. "Say you're sorry to your brother, right now, Mason. You can't go around hitting people for no good reason," I snap, poking him in the chest again.

"Trust me; there was a reason," Malik grumbles, his lips twitching.

Ignoring him, I turn my attention back to Mason, arching my eyebrow. "Now," I yell, causing a few customers to stop what they're doing to watch on.

He folds his arms over his chest and shakes his head. "I'm not fucking saying sorry to him."

"Denny, don't," Max warns, his hand trembling when he reaches for me.

"Don't," I threaten when Mason goes for him again. I turn around, ready to take Max to get some ice, when I catch him smirking smugly at Mason. He soon loses it when he sees me looking.

"It really does hurt, Mase; you should say you're sorry," he whimpers.

Inwardly, I roll my eyes as I walk over to him. I should have known he was playing me for a fool. But he should know by now that I get even.

"Aw, Max, I think we should get this looked at," I tell him sympa-thetically.

He pouts, nodding. "I think he broke something."

"Let me take a closer look," I order gently, gesturing for him to bend down. He leans down, his gaze going to my chest, and I growl, poking the bruise forming under his eye.

He staggers backwards, howling in pain. "What was that for?" he cries.

"One," I snap, holding my finger up, "for trying to make me look like a fucking idiot. Secondly, for doing something to piss Mason off, and third, for staring at my tits again."

"You looked at her tits?" Mason grits out, stepping up behind me so his chest is flush against my back.

"Oh no you don't, Rambo," I warn. "We're going to be late for court."

"Holy shit! Malik, we're going to be late. That's not going to look good if we're late," Harlow cries, rushing over to grab our bags.

As everyone begins to move, I put a hand over my stomach, worried I might not make it through the trial without vomiting again.

CHAPTER
NINE

DENNY

U pon arrival at the courts, I'm immediately guided to a small
room just off from the courtroom I'll be giving my testimony in.

Being alone in the small room that only holds a similar sofa to
what you might use in a conservatory doesn't help my anxiety. I can't
even get through the magazines left to occupy me while I wait to be
called. My nerves have my stomach tied up in knots.

I desperately want to know how Harlow is doing, and what is
going on inside the courtroom. I never expected us to be separated
into different rooms when we arrived. If I did, I would have asked for
an advocate to sit with me since I can't talk to the other witnesses
whilst I'm here. I can't even text Harlow, and if I'm caught doing so, it
could damage the entire case.

Mason had argued to stay with me—hoping they'd make an excep-
tion—but because he's a relative of another witness, he isn't allowed.
They didn't even waver when he said I had been sick. It's hard being
on my own, but I'll do it for Harlow.

Her lawyer stayed with me for a little bit, talking over my testimony, and what I had written in my statement. He didn't need to remind me or prep me. I'll never be able to forget that night or the things he did to her after she arrived at our school.

It still makes me sick how he managed to get away with it for this long. And although I'd never tell Harlow this, a part of me is worried he'll walk free. I have nothing to back it up; it's just a gut feeling.

Getting to my feet, I began to pace the small room, trying to forget about the nausea since my anxiety is fuelling it right now.

A woman's voice plays over the intercom. "Denny Smith, please make your way to Courtroom One."

Oh God.

This is it.

My hands shake as I pull open the door. The security personnel guard is waiting outside for me.

He tips his chin in greeting. "Follow me, Miss Smith," he orders, as he walks through the hallway, not stopping until we reach the end.

My heart races as I stand in front of the double doors. It's beating so fast I'm worried my chest is going to explode. Steeling myself, I push through the doors, coming to a sudden stop when I spot Davis sitting in the defendant box.

My skin crawls at the sight of him. I knew I'd have to see him again. But nothing could have prepared me for it, I realise, as soon as his piercing gaze hits mine. Darkness stares back at me, eyes cold as ice. His lip curls in the corner, a promise of retribution lingering in the air. Acid burns in my throat, as I look away.

If I have to look at him a minute longer, I'm going to make a scene. Now I know why the court has been adjourned so many times. All I want to do is scream 'monster' at him. He should be hung for his crimes.

He's told the courts he's not guilty. And his made-up story didn't stop there. He's accused Malik of being the one to cause bodily assault on Harlow. He claims that he found him beating on her when he caught them in bed together. It doesn't matter that they have eye witnesses placing him at the scene or that he is seen dragging an unconscious Harlow away. He's sticking to his story, and is using reasonable doubt to make the courts believe Harlow is scared of Malik, and therefore, won't speak against him.

The monster has an answer for everything. He even had the audacity to tell them he had no idea what happened to me; that I must have drunk too much and passed out. It's all lies, and hopefully today, I can prove it.

The security guard gestures for me to take the stand. On shaky legs, I climb up onto the platform, folding my hands underneath my stomach.

"Will the accused please rise," the judge announces.

My attention turns to Davis standing, his gaze still on me, danger lurking there. Even now, he is showing his true colours. Black; like his soul. My only hope is that the people in this room are taking notice and see what we do.

If he thinks he can intimidate me, he's lost it, because I'm not going to let him win. Which is why I narrow my gaze on him, daring him to try it. His jaw clenches at my reaction, and he steps forward, bumping into the podium. The guards behind him step forward, pulling him back.

Inhaling, I turn to the judge, keeping my gaze on him like Harlow's lawyer told me to.

They go through the motions where I have to take an oath, swearing to the almighty God to tell the truth, the whole truth, and nothing but the truth. It doesn't mean anything if the person standing here has no soul. These words don't promise truth. They don't promise anything. His sentence is going to be based on the men in this room, and what they decide.

The world will be a safer place without him in it, and I hope they sentence him to life; even if I am praying for death.

As soon as the oath has ended, they don't waste time in getting started.

Davis' defence lawyer stands after closing a file. "Miss Smith, how do you know the defendant?"

"We went to the same school together," I reply, finding it hard to keep my gaze on the judge while answering.

It's the manners I was raised with, and it takes everything not to turn at his voice.

"So, what would you say Mr. Davis and Miss. Evans' relationship was like, Miss. Smith?"

I can't help it, I look at him, rearing back. His question is ludicrous. Harlow's lawyer gives me a subtle nod to answer, so I take a deep breath, turning back to the judge.

"I'm not sure I understand the question. They've never had a relationship of any sort. Not unless you count him bullying her as one," I explain, shrugging.

"So, they were never intimate on any level?"

I shake my head vehemently. "No."

"From my understanding, you were in the same class the day Miss Evan's started school," he states, instead of questioning.

"I was."

"Is it true Miss Evans moved seats on the first day?"

"It is."

"Because the defendant told her to move after she tried to 'feel him up,'" he exclaims, reading off a piece of paper when I turn at the statement.

"No, not at all. That isn't what happened. Harlow had just started. She was in a new environment and hadn't gotten to know anyone. In a rush to get out from everyone's attention, she took the closest empty seat. He made her uncomfortable, so she moved and sat down next to me. She wasn't there long."

"And Miss Evans divulged with you why she moved seats?"

"She did," I tell him.

"And what did she tell you her reasons were, Miss Smith?"

"That he creeped her out. He smelled bad because he hadn't showered and had been doing drugs the night before."

"Speculation," he argues, pointedly looking to the judge. "Continue."

"He tried it on with her and she moved seats. Ever since, he's—"

"Did you see him 'try it on' with her?" he asks, looking up over his glasses.

"No, but I—"

"That's all we need," he retorts, holding his hand up.

I inwardly growl, getting frustrated with his offhanded remarks and rudeness. He isn't letting me finish at all.

Davis—across from me—looks utterly smug. I force back the tears threatening to spill and straighten my spine, not showing them weakness.

"And how close were you sitting to them on that day?"

"I sat at the other end of the classroom," I explain, still struggling to understand why he has started here. We're here about the night he nearly raped her.

"So you would have no idea if Miss Evans' moved of her own free will or because Mr Davis ordered her to?"

"I guess you could state that from my point of view in the room. But there are plenty of other classmates who heard it clear as day. They could backup what Harlow told me, which they did since what happened went around the school that same day. It matched exactly what Harlow told me, so…"

"I see," he murmurs, looking none too happy about my answer. "Let's go over the night of the alleged attack. Can you tell us what happened?"

"We'd just arrived at a party. Harlow and I grabbed a bottle of water from the kitchen then went upstairs to find a bathroom," I begin, rubbing my stomach soothingly. I had found out I was pregnant not days before, and I was still getting sick. I don't want to announce that to the court since I was advised to stick to the events of what happened. "I was sick, and when I came out, Harlow recommended getting some fresh air. We did, but once we hit the stairs, she became flustered. We got outside, and she started to complain she didn't feel right. I went to reach for her to help, when something hard hit me around the head."

I close my eyes when I think of what could have happened if they had hurt me further. Something might have happened to the baby.

"How long were you at the party?"

I just practically answered that! I inwardly growl. "Not long. We had just arrived."

"These parties… they can get rowdy, yes?"

"Yes," I admit.

"Alcohol, drugs?"

I shrug. "I'm not sure about drugs, but there was alcohol there."

"We have a witness who says Miss Evans was drinking heavily. Can you respond?"

I shake my head. "No, she wasn't. She only had water. We both did. And we never left each other's side."

He hums under his breath. "Before you were hit; did you see anyone approach?"

I shake my head. "No."

There's a sour taste in the back of my throat, and my mouth begins to water. *I'm going to be sick.*

And already, I'm drained, my feet aching from standing, but it's nothing compared to the torture the lawyer is putting me through.

"So, you could have fallen and hit your head when you fainted?"

I grip the podium in front of me. "I *didn't* faint. I felt fine, other than I had just been sick. I felt whatever it was they used to knock me out. I assure you, I never passed out."

"Would you say you're close friends with Miss Evans?"

"The best of friends," I reveal.

"And you'd do anything for her?"

"I would," I agree, realising too late that I fell into his trap.

He smirks, looking back down at his sheet. "You were pregnant at the time of the alleged attack, am I right?"

"I was," I tell him.

"Pregnant women faint all the time, Miss Smith. Maybe that's what really happened. You said yourself, you'd do anything for your friend. Lying to protect her should be easy."

"No, you're twisting—"

"I have no further questions, Your Honour," he announces, sitting back down in his chair.

Harlow's lawyer stands, smiling at me encouragingly. I prepare for the onslaught of questions, but I'm surprised to find them easier than the last ones.

He also starts from the beginning, going over Davis's behaviour towards Harlow. He even brings up other transgressions. When he finishes, I feel more confident in his ability to protect Harlow. Davis stands on the other side of the room, but instead of looking at me, he's looking at something behind me. I don't get a chance to see who he's looking at before the security guard is leading me out of the room.

———

W alking outside to the others, they all rush over to me, bombarding me with a million and one questions. None of them look too happy that they have to come back in a couple of days to finish the trial. Harlow didn't get a chance to take the stand.

"How did it go?" Harlow asks, biting her lip.

"They were ruthless. I've never wanted to punch someone so much in my life. His lawyer was savage and uncaring. Yours said not to take it to heart, but I can't help it. I felt like I was the one being accused, not him. And he stood there smug as hell until the end," I grit out. "Luckily, your lawyer knows what he's doing."

"Oh God," Harlow murmurs, collapsing in Malik's arms. "I don't think I can do this. Richard told me about the statement Davis has given to the police. They're going to believe him."

I step up to her, rubbing her arm. "Yeah, but you're telling the truth. Guaranteed somewhere, your lawyer is going to find something that completely disregards his entire statement. They won't believe a word he says then," I assure her. "He thinks he has an answer to everything, even how your first meeting went, but you've got this, Harlow. Your lawyer has this."

Mason wraps an arm around me and pulls me to his side whilst Malik holds Harlow tighter. "Come on; let's get out of here. It's been a long day. We can get some food or something," Mason offers.

"As tired as I am, that sounds so good," I admit, causing him to smile.

Joan heads in our direction, silencing our conversation. She kisses Harlow's head when she reaches us, giving her a sad smile. "I've just finished speaking to Richard. He said you can do a live video link to give your testimony if you think you can't go in there. You won't have to see Davis at all. They'll see you, but you won't see them; you'll only hear the questions."

"That sounds like a good idea," I tell her, wishing they offered that to me.

Harlow bites her lip. "I dunno. I'll think about it. The thought of him watching me and not seeing his reaction, or what he does, creeps me out. It will feel like I'm being spied on," she rushes out, before pouting. "Why can't they just take him out of the room?"

Just then, the doors to the courthouse slam open, and Mason stiffens next to me. Carl, Davis' older brother who is in a gang, paces back and forth, cursing up a blue streak.

His mate taps him on the shoulder, whispering something to him when guards file out, standing to the side to watch them.

I glance at Harlow, who is oblivious, not knowing who they are. When Carl storms away from us, I sag against Mason, but it's short-lived when he stops and turns in our direction.

His lip curls up, matching his brother's from earlier. "Put your lying fucking slut on a lead, Malik," he calls out.

Malik's face turns red. His eyes narrow into slits as he stares murderously into Carl's.

"What the fuck did you just call her?" Malik thunders, stepping forward, but Max, Myles and Mason push him back.

"You heard me. My brother is in there looking at doing some serious fucking time; all for a bitch who can't keep her legs closed."

"Keep telling yourself that, Cam," Max sneers before Malik can open his mouth.

"It's Carl," Carl snaps, shooting daggers at Max.

"Like I care. You could be named Carlie and I wouldn't give a fuck.

What you need to worry about is buying soap-on-a-rope for your brother. A bar of soap won't be good for a rapist in prison," he snarls.

When Carl rushes forward, the security guards move away from the wall and intercept him before he can reach us.

"Why don't we go?" Myles suggests, and I shakily nod, agreeing with him.

I want this day to be over.

CHAPTER
TEN

DENNY

I bolt upright at the sound of something smashing on the floor. With my mind foggy, still half asleep, I take a deep breath and lie back down.

It was just a dream.

I hate it when you dream of something and could have sworn it was real, and with the events of today still hounding me, I'm not surprised it's happened.

Even now, after waking up seconds ago, my thoughts are immediately plagued with the court case. I went to bed thinking about it and then fell asleep, only to dream about it. I can't catch a break from it.

I'm exhausted—emotionally and physically. Instead of coming home to rest and order in, we went out for food then headed back to Harlow's. By the time Mason picked up on my tiredness, I was completely done in. He drove me home, kissed me on the cheek, then left, promising he would see me tomorrow.

I didn't do anything other than shower before I fell into bed, falling into a deep slumber.

Until now.

Rolling onto my back, I stare up at the ceiling, the moon casting an eerie shadow over the light. Needing a glass of water or a warm glass of milk, I sit up, swiping my hair out of my face with a yawn.

My bare feet hit the carpet and a chill runs up my spine at the cool breeze skirting around the floor. Shaking it off as I know I'll be back in bed within a few minutes, I walk over to the door.

My hand grips the door handle, pushing it down, when glass shatters from somewhere in the house. I freeze, my heartrate skyrocketing as I listen for anything else.

When I don't hear anything, I stupidly pull the door open, my breath hitching when the moonlight shines through the blinds, luminating a figure coming through the living room window.

My breath hitches when I see the light reflect off something shiny in the person's hand. Coming unglued, I quickly shut the door as quietly as I can. A small cry passes through my lips when it makes a clicking noise, echoing over the pulse in my ears. I quietly turn the lock, locking it.

I suck in a breath, holding it in as I rest my head against the door, wondering what to do. My heart is beating rapidly against my ribcage, and my vision is beginning to blur.

Someone is inside the house.

I glance around the room, trying to find somewhere to hide, but there isn't anywhere safe enough for me to fit my bump. And there's no way I'll get out the bedroom window without hurting myself in the process.

Hearing another loud crash, followed by a quiet curse, I whimper. I slap my hand over my mouth, feeling tears leak from my eyes.

"Fucking bitch! Where are you?" I hear, as a door close by is kicked open.

I vaguely recognise the voice, but I can't think over the constant buzz in my ears.

Glancing around the room once again—but for a weapon this time —my gaze lands on a magazine, one I had been reading the other night. I begin to tear pages out of the book, folding them up into thick blocks, and bend down to shove them under the door. It will be harder for him to push it open if they're wedged there.

It's a trick I learned when my mother refused to let me have a lock on my bedroom door. It worked, but she also wasn't out to kill me. Once that's done, I shakily get to my feet, nearly falling back when he bangs his fist on the door. It shakes from the force, and I whimper, looking for something else to use.

"Open up now, you slut!" he snarls, this time putting on an accent. I'm not sure how I know, but I do. His voice doesn't sound the same as before, and I don't think there are two people out there.

In a daze, I walk backwards, away from the door, and my back bumps into the chest of drawers. With wide eyes, I quickly drag them over to the door, glad there isn't much in there. I tip it back, letting it thud against door. Just to make sure it stays, I throw my suitcase over the top, sighing with relief when the chest of drawers stay slanted.

When he begins to kick the door, I whimper and step away. My entire body shakes as I stare, unblinking, at the door, hoping like hell the paper and drawers are enough to keep him out.

I want Mason.

I need...

Police!

I need to call the police. Racing over to the bed, I grab my phone off charge, dialling nine-nine-nine.

I glance back to the door as it rings in my ear, screaming when a large knife slices through the wood. It wiggles around in the hole he's created, and I take that moment to crouch down beside the wardrobe, squeezing between it and the wall.

"Nine-nine-nine, what's your emergency?"

"Police, please. I have an intruder in my home," I whisper. I'm not sure why I'm whispering. He knows I'm in here. But it feels safe. Sensible.

My entire body aches from shaking so hard, my fingers gripping the phone like a vice.

"Okay, Miss. Can you tell us where you are?"

I rattle off the address before letting them know I'm pregnant, and that I'm scared for my baby's safety.

"I'm twenty-seven weeks pregnant and he has a knife," I cry, a sob tearing from my throat when the knife is pulled out of the door.

"Calm down. We have dispatched officers to the address. They are two minutes out," she explains, calm as can be. "Is there anyone else in the house with you?"

"It's me and whoever is trying to get to me," I tell her through sobs.

The door rattles again, causing a scream to tear from my throat. This time I don't bother to mask the sound, not when I see the knife slice through the door again, making the original hole bigger.

"Please, please, help me. He's going to get in," I wail, curling my knees up as close as they'll reach me.

I begin to rock, and I don't stop, not even when I see flashing blue lights. He stops suddenly, and I hear scratching of some kind near the door, before I hear another window smash in the next room.

I can't breathe.

A commotion at the front door causes me to whimper. "Police!" is yelled through the bungalow.

I relax against the wall, tears streaming down my face, before I get up and race to the door.

"I'm in here. I'm in here," I call out, moving the chest of drawers.

I step on something and kneel down, picking up the glossy paper. I freeze, ignoring the police outside the door, who are telling me to stay put until they search the premises.

I shine the light from my phone onto the paper, reading the words written in blue ink. 'This is what happens to grasses'.

Does that mean he's coming back?

A hiccup a sob, turning the paper over. It takes me a moment to register what I'm seeing, but the second I do, a blood curling scream tears from my throat. I stagger backwards, tripping over my suitcase and landing on my arse, pain shooting up my spine.

"No. No. No."

"Miss, please let the officers in," I hear from the phone clutched between my fingers.

NO! NO!

I clench my eyes shut, but the image is still there, seared into my brain. "No, no, no, no. It's not real. It's not real," I chant to myself.

"Miss," the woman calls out, louder this time.

"I need to go. I need to go," I tell her, ending the call. I'm not sure who I'm calling; I just call the last person in my phone before the nine-nine-nine call.

"Hello?" Harlow answers, her voice filled with sleep.

I cry out at the sound of her voice, needing that safety. "Harlow, help me. Please! Help me! I need to get out of here. It's not safe. Please," I wail, my voice rising. "Please!"

"Denny? Denny? Calm down. What's going on? Are you okay?" she asks. "Malik, wake up!"

I open my mouth to answer, but I scream at the sound of wood splintering. I crawl backwards, shoving myself back into the corner, curling my legs to my chest, panting heavily.

The photo creases in my hand as I stare at it, rocking backwards and forwards. I can barely see it through my tears, but it doesn't matter. The image is burned into my mind.

Please no! Please don't let it be true.

Hannah lies motionless on the dirty floor, her bruised body covered in dirt, her face cut and bloody. Her eyes are what petrify me. They're staring blankly at the camera. I know she's dead, but for some reason, I can feel the tortured soul staring back at me. I can see the scared look in her dilated pupils.

The bottom half of her clothes are missing, and there's blood pooled between her legs. The word 'rat' is carved above her pubic bone.

I swivel to the side, puking up on the carpet beside me, before resting my head against my knees.

Why would they do this to her? Is that what he has planned for me? Feeling sicker by the second, I block out all the loud voices around me and the banging on the bedroom door, too afraid to move.

My stomach clenches painfully as I heave in and out with my cries.

I'm so consumed with fear, I don't hear them break into the room. It isn't until a hand reaches out for me that I react.

I scream, slapping the hands away from me. "Don't touch me! Don't touch me!"

"Miss, let us look you over," a kind woman's voice pleads.

"No!" I scream until my voice is hoarse.

"We need to sedate her," I hear said.

"I'm her boyfriend," I hear roared, before there's a commotion outside the door.

Mason.

I look up in time to see him skid across the floor, collapsing to his knees beside me, not caring that he's now covered in sick.

When he reaches for me, I break out of my trance and dive at him. I wrap my hand around his neck, a whimper slipping through my lips at the sharp pain in my stomach.

"Mason," I croak out, my voice hoarse.

"Yeah, baby, it's me. Will you let me carry you out so the paramedics can take a look at you?" he asks softly.

I tilt my head up, lines creasing my forehead, before I take in the room, seeing two paramedics standing close by.

I cling to him, shoving my face into his neck as my stomach tightens. "Did they get him?"

"Get who?" he asks, his body tightening. "Did someone hurt you?"

He lifts me up and sits me down on the bed. When he tries to let go, I shake my head, and he takes a seat next to me.

When the paramedics steps closer, I dig my nails into his hand. "He's going to kill me."

"Who?" he growls.

"They killed Hannah, and they'll come for me too. I think they raped her. They were going to do that to me," I tell him, becoming hysterical. "He's going to do that to me. He was right out there. He gave me this." I crumple the photo in my hand, a fresh wave of pain hitting me low in the stomach.

"Shush, babe. It's going to be okay. I promise," he tells me, lifting my chin until I'm looking directly into his chocolate-coloured eyes. I know he's putting on a brave face. I can see behind the façade. He's scared too. "Let the paramedics check you over and then you can tell me the rest. I swear."

"It hurts," I breathe out, finally registering just how bad the cramps are.

He jerks his chin to the paramedics behind me and they rush over to check me out. When one touches my stomach, I nearly collapse.

The paramedics share a look. I shake my head, wiping the tears from my cheeks. "What's wrong?"

"We need to get you to the hospital," the paramedic explains, gathering her stuff.

I glance to Mason, my eyes wide. "What's wrong? Is it the baby? Did I do something?" I ask, my voice rising. "Please, what's going on?"

Mason wraps his arm around me and presses a kiss to my head. "Tell us," he demands, his voice clogged with emotion.

She places her hands on her knees, her expression somewhat tight. "We can't be too sure. Her heartrate is high and she seems to be contracting, but due to the night's events, we can't be sure if it's all the stress Mum and Baby have been through that is causing it. We would like to get her checked out," she explains gently.

"It's too early," Mason growls.

"Please no," I breathe out, guilt consuming me.

The redheaded paramedic walks in with a chair, but Mason stands, pulling me into his arms. "I've got her," he rushes out, and I grip his neck, crying out as another cramp hits me.

When we get outside, the cool air feels good against my skin. I lean back, surprised to find Harlow and the others being held back by police officers.

"Oh my god, is she okay?" Harlow cries. "What happened?"

Mason steps into the ambulance, placing me down on the bed before turning to them. "I'll explain at the hospital. They're taking her to St. George's, so meet us there," he explains, as I clutch my stomach, sweat beading at my forehead.

It isn't time.

Harlow collapses into Malik's waiting arms, tears streaming down her face. "She can't have the baby yet. It's too early. We read a book about birth. It's too early." I hear her go on as the doors shut behind the paramedic.

I glance up at her when she starts placing stuff on my chest, hooking me up to a machine. "Please make it stop," I plead.

I can't have her now. Not when she's this premature. I can't lose her. The thought is more terrifying than tonight's events.

My heart sinks. I did this to her. Instead of staying calm, I lost it. I could be the reason my baby is in danger.

An oxygen mask is placed over my mouth, and I start sucking in deep breaths, my head becoming woozy. I relax against the bed, the pain in my stomach beginning to ease as my eyes begin to droop.

The last thing I remember is Mason taking my hand, giving it a light squeeze.

———

I groggily come to at the hospital, my heart racing when I see a doctor walk through, pushing a scan machine.

Mason grips my hand when I begin to shake. "They just want to check over the baby," he assures me.

"I'm Doctor Harold, and I'll be treating you this evening. Can you tell me where the pain is?"

I point to the bottom of my stomach, grimacing as another contraction hits me. "Please help my baby," I plead.

"Why don't we take a quick look and see what's going on?" he murmurs, moving a strap that is wrapped around my stomach. I glance to Mason, my eyes pleading with him to answer.

"They're to monitor the baby's heartbeat, and the contractions."

I nod, squeezing his hand as the doctor squirts gel over my stomach. When the nurse walks in, he doesn't look away from what he is doing.

He puts the sensor down before rubbing alcohol rub over his hands. "Everything seems okay with the baby, but I'd like to have a cervix exam done. We need to see if you're dilated or not. Would you prefer a female doctor?"

I shake my head. At this point, a monk could do it and I wouldn't care. I just want my baby to be okay.

"I don't mind," I assure him, then spend the next ten minutes or so being poked and prodded in the most intimate of places.

Once he's done and cleaned up, he comes to stand beside me next to the bed. "Your cervix is still intact. You aren't dilated," he reveals, and I relax somewhat. "Your man here explained what happened tonight. I believe the stress caused you to have Braxton hicks. The contractions can be painful, but it's your body's way of preparing itself to deliver."

"So, I'm not going to go into labour?" I breathe out, clenching my eyes as a few tears slip free.

"No. We would like to monitor you for a while longer, and if all is okay, you're free to go home."

"That's it?" Mason asks, standing up. "She's okay? The baby is okay?"

"Yes, both Mum and Baby are doing fine, considering."

"Is there anything we should do when we leave?" he asks, gripping my hand.

"I'd advise you to take it easy for the next couple of days," he says, addressing me now. "Try to keep off your feet and don't do anything too strenuous."

"I'll make sure she does," Mason announces.

"I'll leave you in your nurse's care," the doctor announces, before pulling back the curtain and leaving.

Mason slumps against the bedrail, bringing my hand up to his lips, his eyes glassy with tears. "I was so fucking scared," he rasps.

The look in his eyes is so powerful. I can't explain it. I just feel it. He was petrified, and not just for the baby. It was for me.

My shoulders shake as I silently cry. "You came for me."

"I'll always come for you," he promises, his voice cracking.

I reach over, running my finger down his cheek. "Hey, it's okay."

He forces out a laugh. "It's far from okay, Denny. I could have lost you both tonight."

I whimper, closing my eyes for a moment. "Don't."

"Are you okay?"

I shake my head. "I'm not sure how to deal with it. I'm just relieved the baby is okay. Did the police get him?"

"I don't know. I've not left the room. Malik messaged me to say they were here, but let's not think about that right now. Let's concentrate on you."

"They're here?" I ask, my voice filled with emotion.

"Malik and the rest?" he asks, and I nod. "They're all in the waiting area. And before you say anything, they aren't leaving until you do."

"But I am," I tell him, watching as his forehead creases. "I can't stay here. Not now. I'm not safe."

"You are staying," he growls. "You aren't leaving me."

"Mason, he was going to…" I swallow bile, unable to form the words.

"I'm sorry. So fucking sorry I couldn't protect you, Denny. But you can't leave me."

"Mason," I say softly, squeezing his hand. "This wasn't your fault. You couldn't have predicted this would happen."

"I should have been there."

"I can't go back there, Mason. Don't make me. Not after tonight. I need to go back to my nan's."

"No, you need to come home with me. Where you belong," he demands, his eyes glistening with tears.

"I'm not moving in with you."

"Yes, Denny, you are."

"I'm not," I reply with a bite to my tone.

He arches an eyebrow with a 'we'll see' look, but I ignore him, closing my eyes as tiredness begins to seep in.

CHAPTER
ELEVEN

DENNY

I t has been three weeks since the break-in and a lot has changed during that time. After being released from hospital, I tried to call Nan to warn her I was coming home, and to fill her in on what happened, but Mason snatched the phone off me and told her exactly what was happening.

I was moving in with him, and I wasn't going back.

To my dismay, my nan agreed, informing him she had already packed up my stuff and was getting it shipped over.

When I tried to argue, she informed me it would be pointless going back when she had bought a house over here. I didn't have an argument after that, but I was secretly thrilled we wouldn't be apart. I love my nan, and never want to be away from her again.

Still, I refused to move in with Mason at first. Instead, I took Malik's old bedroom and stayed there. However, after two weeks of listening to Mason grovel and plead, I gave in.

Today is the first day in our new home, but I'm not ready to get up. My legs are still sore from the long day yesterday. When Mason found out I still had stuff over at my parents, he wanted to get it. I tried to tell him it had all probably long been burnt to a crisp, but he didn't care.

My mother wasn't there when we arrived, but my dad looked pleased to see me. He rushed to explain how he had boxed the rest of my things up and hid them in the cellar so she wouldn't find them.

I just gave Mason a look that said, 'I told you so'.

We managed to get most of it in the boot of Mason's car before she pulled up in her flashy motor, wearing her over-the-top fancy clothes. She hadn't even shut the car before she went crazy, demanding we leave her property before she called the police. If Dad hadn't stopped her by reminding her the neighbours would talk with police on their doorstep, she would have called them. The second Dad gave me a silent look that said 'go', I hightailed it out of there. After everything that had happened, she was the last thing on my list to deal with.

Now that the decorating is done and the furniture is fitted, and my boxes have arrived, there's no more excuses as to why I can't move in.

I run a hand through my hair. I want this. I can't deny it. I don't know why I'm making this harder on Mason. He has done nothing but be a gentleman the past few weeks and has taken care of me since I was released from hospital. I couldn't have asked for anything more.

There's just something holding me back.

And it isn't attraction. In fact, my attraction towards him has heightened to the point I can't be alone with him. My entire body burns for him, craving him so deeply sometimes that I feel like my heart will stop if I don't get it.

And tonight, we will be sharing a bed.

It's going to be torture having him so close. Up until now, he has respected my boundaries by staying in his own room. But what will happen when we are alone, with no other soul in the house, and we are in bed? My mind runs wild with all the things I want to do to him.

The bedroom door creaks open, and I look up, finding Mason.

He grins. "Hey, you're already awake."

I lift the blanket up over my chest, conscious of the fact I'm only wearing knickers and one of his T-shirts, which I have been robbing every night to sleep in. I can't help it. They smell like him, and it makes me feel safe.

"Um, yeah. Why wouldn't I be?" I ask, hoping he can't see that I'm blushing.

I was thinking about him, imagining all the dirty things we could do together, and then he walked in. It seems like fate.

"You're normally awake by now, wanting breakfast. I didn't want to wake you though. I know yesterday was hard for you," he explains. "Max went to the chippy, so if you want some, hurry up before he eats it."

My stomach grumbles and I lick my lips. "I could eat," I tell him. "What time is it?"

I look around for my phone, but his next words stop me. "It's half twelve."

My lips part as I stare up at him. "Half twelve? Are you kidding me? I've been asleep for fourteen hours?"

"It's fine," he assures me, waving me off. "Even Joan agreed with me when the others said to wake you. Max was moaning about you being able to sleep but he wasn't; blah, blah, blah. Anyway, she explained that in a few months, it will be you who isn't able to have a lie in, so we should all let you now."

"She could be a good baby," I defend, rubbing my stomach before sliding out of bed.

I grab a pair of maternity jeans and a loose-hanging T-shirt before scanning the room for my pumps. Now my feet are less swollen, I want to wear them.

Seeing them under the chair next to the desk, I lean down and grab them. I hear a groan behind me and shoot up, turning to find Mason's heated gaze directed at my arse. I blush, realising I just gave him a nice view of my red lace maternity knickers.

He rubs the back of his neck, taking a step backwards and bumping into the door. "I'll um... I'll just go wait at ours. See you there," he rushes out, his gaze going to my crotch once again.

Once he's stumbled his way out of the room, a laugh escapes me.

At least my fears he would start to find me unattractive are unwarranted. I have been putting more weight on over the past few weeks, and I was worried it would turn him off. Although, I have to say, after spending my life all skin and bone, it's nice to have some shape to me.

I quickly race over to the bathroom across the hall, wanting to be ready before the food arrives. Although the brothers doted on me the first week after being released from the hospital, it didn't last. Not that they don't take care of me; they do. But it's food. It's like gold in this house. If you have it, they want it.

It's got to the point where I have to make my own food behind their backs just so Max and Mason can't rob it.

My brother moved out of our family home as soon as he could, and before that, we never really shared dinners together. Only formal ones like Christmas and birthdays. So I'm still technically learning how to live with a house full of men.

But I'm approaching my last nerve, and it will soon snap if they keep me away from my food.

And if I hear 'sharing is caring' one more time, I'm going to blow a gasket.

Walking over to the house once I'm dressed, I take in all the boxes stacked up outside the front door of our little makeshift patio.

My stomach swirls with anticipation. I haven't shown it, not wanting to let Mason know he won, but I'm secretly excited about having our own place.

The front door is already open, so I step inside, marvelling at the warm brown and green painted on the walls. The sofa is a lighter shade of brown, decorated with pillows that are a lighter green than the wall.

Harlow gave a lot of input when it came to decorating, and she did good. It's something I would have picked out for myself. It's fresh and modern, yet homey. Even the ornaments and lightshade match the décor.

I chuckle at the sight of the large TV hanging on the wall. I shouldn't be surprised at the size, though I don't understand it. It isn't a large room, so having it that big would soon enough cause a trip to the opticians.

Seeing the home for the first time, and how much he's accomplished here, brings tears to my eyes. When he started picking colours, he had no idea that I'd come back or if I'd even say yes. And yet he did it, that sure we would end up together.

Harlow walks in, grinning from ear to ear. "What do you think?"

"It looks amazing," I admit.

"Thank God," she breathes out. "Mason has been on my back, worrying he's done something wrong." She pulls me in for a hug before pulling back. "How are you? You've been sleeping a lot more lately. I was starting to worry we wouldn't see you at all today."

"Yeah, I'm doing okay. I think it's the heat making me tired, but it's starting to cool down now so hopefully that eases off."

"Hopefully," she replies. "Let's go see where Mason is so he can give you a tour."

I nod and follow her into the kitchen. Mason is there, standing over a box, going through its contents. When I see what box it is, I pale. "Hey! What the hell are you doing?"

He startles, jumping back from the box. When he sees me, he grins, but it slips when he notices how unhappy I am. "Um… What does it look like I'm doing?"

"It looks like you're going through my personal belongings. One, I might add, has in bold black ink *not* to open unless you're Denny," I tell him, arching an eyebrow.

The box is filled with diaries and other personal items. But it's what's at the bottom of the box that has my anxiety spiking.

"I didn't know it was yours. I didn't see your name," he replies, a faint blush rising in his cheeks.

"Well, now you do, so get your paws out of there," I warn.

"Hey, bro, you'd better not have fucking woke Denny up," Max yells, startling me. He rounds the corner, entering the kitchen, and comes to a sudden stop. "Denny, hey. Shit. I was just telling Mason that he'd better not have woken you up. I knew you needed the rest, and you know what he's like. We were gonna bring you a plate of food in bed."

I keep staring at him, and he whimpers, turning to Mason. "Mason…"

He is such a liar. He doesn't want me around. He's fed up of me. It probably won't be long until the rest are too.

"I'm not hungry anyway," I mutter, lying. I need to get out of here. I move out of the kitchen and back into the front room, where I take a seat on the sofa. Tears gather in my eyes.

The others follow. Mason takes one look at me and rounds on his brother. "What the fuck, Max?" he growls, slapping him across the head.

He rubs the spot, wincing. "Sorry, man," Max groans, before taking a step towards me. "It's okay, Denny. There's plenty of food to go around for all of us."

Oh, so it isn't about me at all, but about him being worried about losing food. I know I've been eating more than normal, but I didn't think I was that bad. It's them who keep stealing all my food.

Or at least, it was.

Still, I'm livid. How dare he? How dare they?

This morning flashes in my mind, and I whimper. Maybe Mason didn't run out because he was attracted to me, maybe it was because he was repulsed by me.

I know I'm being irrational, but I don't care.

"It's fine, Max," I grit out, seconds away from either crying or having a screaming fit.

"Ahh shit, you're going to cry," Max states, taking two steps away from me.

I glare up at him, ignoring my nose stinging and my throat swelling. "No, I'm not," I snap.

I'm pretty sure my lip just trembled.

"Yes, you are," he points out, just as Mason bravely takes a seat next to me.

"Are you okay, angel?"

Why is he being nice all of a sudden? Does he think I'm weak? "I'm fine," I growl. "It's not the end of the world if I skip one meal, Mason. I *can* reject food if I want to. It's not like I'm going to waste away, *is it*." I inhale, my voice getting higher when I continue. "I mean, I wouldn't want to starve the rest of you."

Harlow takes a seat on the other side of me, running her hand down my back. "He didn't mean it like that, babe."

I sniffle, ducking my head. "It's what they're all thinking. Max can't stand to eat in the same room with me because he thinks I'm going to eat all his food," I explain, my voice hitching.

"Denny," Harlow whispers.

"No. Don't try to stick up for them," I tell her, watching as Max takes another step back. "And now to top it off, Mason thinks I'm fat."

As soon as the last word escapes my mouth, I wrap my arms around her, shoving my face into her neck as I cry hysterically.

"Mason, I can't believe you would think that," Harlow snaps, her body tensing.

"I never said she was fat," he blurts out, confusion in his tone.

I snap my head around to him. "But you thought it. You're repulsed by me. Running off as soon as you see me half naked."

"When did I see you half naked?" he asks, taken aback.

"Dude... burn!" Max yells, laughing. When I glance at him, he frowns, his lips tipping down. "I'll, um, shut up."

Maverick and Myles step into the room, both of them taking in the scene.

"What's happened? Who the fuck upset Denny?" Maverick snaps, his eyes narrowing on each person.

"Bro, you don't want to get involved," Max warns.

"You all think I'm fat," I wail, feeling like I've just stepped onto the crazy train.

I'm not even sure where it's all coming from. I know I'm acting crazy, but I just can't stop it.

"Who said she was fat?" Myles asks, his face tightening with anger.

"Can everyone clear out a minute and let me talk to Denny alone?"

"I don't think that's a good idea," Max warns with a mouth full of sausage.

I hadn't even noticed the bags in Maverick's hand or that Max now had one open.

"That sausage is going to be shoved somewhere other than your mouth if you don't fuck off," Mason growls.

One by one, they begin to leave. Harlow stays behind, staring down at me. "Will you be okay?" she asks softly.

I nod, wiping my runny nose with the back of my hand before wiping it on the back of Mason's jeans.

"Please tell me you didn't just do that, Denny," he pleads, sounding disgusted, which in turn sets me off again.

Harlow goes to comfort me, but Mason gives her a warning look that has her retreating and following the others.

They're probably in the kitchen eating all my food. Just smelling the salt and vinegar has my stomach growling and my tastebuds watering.

"What's going on, Denny?"

"Nothing. It's just the pregnancy hormones," I lie, feeling foolish.

I close my eyes. *I just wiped snot all over his jeans.*

They're good jeans too.

"Bullshit. I can piss a better excuse than that," he remarks crudely.

I sniffle, looking away. "It's not an excuse."

"Tell. Me. What's. Wrong, before I go Jessica Fletcher on your arse and find out for myself."

"Jessica Fletcher?" I question, scrunching up my nose.

"Um… Yeah. My nan used to make me watch it as a kid, okay," he rushes out, holding his hands up.

I watch him closely. "And you liked it?"

"You're kidding, right? I loved it. She was a bad-arse detective," he gushes, before blanking his expression. "It was okay, I suppose."

"You suppose?" I tease, amused.

"Stop changing the subject," he snaps, and I raise my brow at him. "Tell me why you're so upset."

I throw my hands up, yelling, "Because you're disgusted by me."

"You're seriously having me on right now. Please tell me you are, Denny, because this isn't a joke," he warns, shuffling closer, resting his hand over my thigh.

"No," I whisper, watching as my tears soak into my jeans.

"Look at me," he demands. When I don't comply, he grips my chin gently, tilting my head up until I'm facing him. The lines around his eyes soften. "When have I ever given you the impression I thought you were fat, angel?"

"Earlier, in the bedroom. You took one look at me and hightailed it out of there," I tell him, feeling my cheeks heat. "Then you and Max have been conspiring against me and my food. It's because you think I'm fat. You don't want me putting more weight on. It hurts. I know you're going to work each night and probably banging some skinny-arse bitch who doesn't have a large stomach, who doesn't have stretchmarks or cellulite."

His blank expression and his lack of response only confirm it's true. He's just too scared to admit it. The coward is probably thinking of a way to let me down gently.

I hadn't even known I felt that way until the words were spilling out of my mouth.

And now he knows.

And he isn't saying anything.

Tears gather in my eyes, and when I stare up at him, his lips tighten, right before he bursts out laughing.

What?

I narrow my gaze on him. "Why the hell are you laughing?"

"Let's start with this morning," he begins, smothering his laughter. "I rushed out of there because I know you aren't ready for me. I want you. *You!* So badly it hurts to be around you."

"But—"

"And as for cheating, I'd never do that to you. Ever. There is no one else. I thought I had proved that to you."

I duck my head, wringing my fingers together. "But we aren't together."

"Yes, we are," he growls.

"We're not, and you did it before," I remind him, feeling guilty when his expression falls.

"No, Denny, I didn't. Yes, I fucked up. I know there's nothing I can do to take it all back. But please, give me a chance to repair what I broke. Give me a chance to prove to you I'm not that person. Not with you. Never with you," he pleads.

"I'm sorry," I whisper.

"No, don't be. I'm the one who caused you to doubt me. But don't doubt me now. We're together. And I mean it."

"You don't think I'm unattractive?"

He arches a brow, reaching for my wrist. "Would this happen if I did?"

He places my hand over his cock, and I inhale when I find it hard. "What?" I murmur, squeezing my knees together.

"I'm always hard for you, Denny. The only reason I haven't taken you already is because I know you aren't ready. And I know I have a lot to make up for, so I want to do this right. I want us to work, and I don't want sex complicating that. Not yet," he tells me, a devilish smirk reaching his lips at his last words.

My shoulders sag. "You'll get bored, Mason. You'll see. I'm nothing special."

He presses a kiss to my forehead. "I never make promises, Denny. I had a childhood filled with broken ones that taught me never to make ones I couldn't keep. But I'm promising you now, that is one thing that will never happen when it comes to you," he tells me, his voice fierce. "And Denny, angel, you are special. I'll spend eternity showing you how special if you let me."

My lips part, and he takes advantage, leaning forward to press his lips against mine. I moan, tasting him as he thrusts his tongue inside my mouth.

I run my hand up his strong, muscled bicep, pressing closer as I seek more. He groans low in his throat, gripping the back of my neck, controlling the kiss.

A throat clears and I pull back, pressing my fingers to my lips. I can still feel him, still taste him.

"Mase, the lawyer is here, and he needs to see you both. He's in the kitchen," Maverick explains.

The blood drains from my face and I grip Mason's hand, our kiss forgotten. He tucks a strand of hair behind my ear. "It's going to be okay."

Maverick pauses in the doorway, turning back to us. "And Denny? Ignore Max. He's territorial over his food and he's just scared he's met his match. It's nothing personal."

"I guess," I murmur.

"Also, whilst I have you alone, your nan should be arriving too."

"My nan?" I ask, my eyebrows nearly hitting my hairline. "How do you know that?"

He winks. "I grabbed her number from Harlow."

He leaves the room and Mason turns to me, lines creasing his forehead. "Are you okay? I can tell the lawyer to come back."

"No, we can't ignore him," I tell him.

"Yeah, but you've been through a lot."

"I know, but it's not going to go away," I remind him, before muttering, "Even if I do pray every night."

"Alright, but the minute I see it's getting to you, I'm asking him to leave."

I nod, letting him help me up off the sofa.

It will be okay.

It will.

CHAPTER
TWELVE

DENNY

Mason and I step into the kitchen, finding Harlow's lawyer—Richard Cole—sitting at the breakfast bar, his briefcase on the worktop.

Ominous thoughts squirm in my mind at his unexpected arrival. Is he here to confirm what I already know, which is that Hannah is dead? And if he is, have the police managed to recover her remains?

Yet, as important as those things are, I feel guilty for hoping he's here to tell me they found the culprit who broke into my brother's home. It's been hard to forget that night, and how close I was to losing our unborn baby. The only reason I've stayed sane and relaxed is because I'm no longer alone. I have Mason and his brothers looking out for me.

Maverick—probably sensing my mood—meets my gaze. With one look, he lets me know I've got this, and he's got my back. All the brothers are like this. They can make you feel like anything is possible with one glance. No words are shared, but you feel them like they're spoken. Mason shares the same soulful eyes, yet when he looks at me, I feel like he can see right into my soul.

Joan and Mark are huddled to the side of the breakfast bar, where Malik and Harlow stand anxiously waiting to hear what Richard has to say.

"I'm sure you're all guessing why I called you here today," Richard announces, looking from Harlow to Malik, before his attention lands on me.

We are. We have a meeting already scheduled for a few days, so whatever he has to say must be urgent if he can't wait until then.

"Talk," Malik orders, pulling Harlow against his chest.

He pushes his glasses up the brim of his nose. "A new witness has come forward with what could be vital evidence for our case."

Harlow steps forward, placing her hands over the counter. "Who?" she trembles.

Mason grabs my attention, arching his brow in question. I shrug, having no clue either. There was no one else there the night Harlow got attacked.

Or was there, and that's why he's here?

No, there definitely wasn't.

I clear my throat before informing him, "No one else was there, Richard. They would have come forward by now. He wasn't well liked."

Myles shakes his head. "Not necessarily. It could be one of his friends coming forward."

Richard takes out a legal pad, scribbling something down. "This isn't regarding the case Harlow has filed. This is a new claim against him, but he'll be tried at the same time for both. He's been trying to claim reasonable doubt against Harlow's testimony, but with the new witness coming forward, we're able to prove he's a repeat offender."

"Who?" I demand.

"I'm not at liberty to say," he explains, grimacing. "The witness is being held in protective custody until the trial."

"And what about the break-in?" Mason asks, pulling me against his chest.

"The police have still not managed to locate Miss Gittens. They are still looking. Her case is now a pending murder investigation, but I'm sorry, I don't have any more information on the subject."

"And the break-in?" Mason demands again. "He could have killed her."

Richard addresses me as he replies, "With the photograph of Miss Gittens and the break-in, and what you said in your statement, the police are certain that whoever murdered Miss Gittens is targeting witnesses. I happen to believe this is true, which is why the witness has been put into protective custody. From here on out, you must be very vigilant, Miss Smith."

My worst fears have come to light. For weeks now, I have been lying to myself, believing it was just a coincidence that I was broken into the day of my testimony. But it's not. My nightmare is connected to the trail.

I clutch my stomach, feeling nauseated.

I wish I could unsee the picture that still haunts me. But I can't. And now I have a new image in my mind now it has been confirmed. Every night I go to sleep, I'll be petrified of what might happen in my nightmares. I already pictured Hannah's death in a million and one ways. I picture my death the night he broke in. I even lived through the nightmare of my own baby's death. And although I woke up each time, the emotions, the heart attack, the pure fear… it ran through my veins.

Someone is going to kill me.

"No!" Harlow cries, coming out of her shock. "It can't be true. Please tell me it's not true."

Richard's expression morphs into one of pity and sadness. "I'm sorry, Harlow, but it's true."

"When? When did this happen? What's the evidence?" she pleads, losing her breath. "I need to know. Please."

"Babe, calm down," Malik orders gently, wrapping his arms tightly around her when she begins to take fast, deep breaths.

She pulls back, looking up at him with tears running down her cheeks. "I can't. If he's raped someone else, I need to know. It's my fault. Don't you see that? If I had gone to the police sooner about him instead of worrying about making the situation worse, we wouldn't be standing here right now."

"I disagree," Richard adds, frowning. "The police wouldn't have charged him if they only had hearsay as evidence; they would need solid proof to arrest him, Harlow. You would never have had that if you went to them with concerns."

"It shouldn't be this way," Mark growls. "She shouldn't have to wait to be attacked for something to be done."

"I couldn't agree with you more, sir, but the law is the law I'm afraid," he replies. "But Harlow has the evidence to put Mr Davis away for a long time." He turns to Harlow, giving her a small smile. "You are taking a stand. That's what matters right now."

Joan steps up beside Harlow, running a hand down her arm. "Look at it this way, my girl; by standing up, you are saving more innocent girls from being hurt."

"We can't know that," Harlow whispers. "We can't know it will go in my favour. He could be free to do this again."

I hate to be the one to say it, and I know I should be positive right now, but I'm scared. "What if he does get away with it? He's claiming a pretty good alibi. He's mixing the truth with lies," I tell him, before pointing at Malik. "You can see yourself how protective Malik is. It's not a smothering protectiveness. He's doing it out of love. He'd never lay a hand on her. And you've known Harlow awhile, so you know she'd never cheat."

"I know this. And this is what we have to prove to the courts."

I sigh, sinking back into Mason, using him for support.

"Please, Richard. Please tell us something; anything," Harlow pleads. "I can't stand not knowing who the witness is or what happened to them. Did it happen after me?"

"Is there nothing you can tell them to put their minds at rest?" Joan asks.

Sighing, Richard takes stock of everyone in the room, his shoulders deflating. "Alright, alright," he gives in. "I'm not allowed to mention names, so please don't ask me to."

"We won't," I promise, squeezing Mason's hand.

"The witness came forward a few days ago and filed an official complaint. With her, she had a bag of clothes she was wearing the night of the rape. We also have a hospital report confirming her story," he explains, before letting out a sigh. "I'm going to be honest with you, I don't have all the facts. I don't know if we can prove it was Mr Davis who, in fact, raped her."

"Why now?" Harlow asks, wiping away tears.

"In my line of work, I see a lot of cases go the same way. Victims are scared to step forward. I believe this is the same case for this witness. It happened years ago, but I believe you coming forward gave her the courage."

When he pauses, looking unsure if he should say the next bit, Malik speaks up. "What?"

"Like Harlow, I believe this girl is feeling unnecessary guilt."

"She's blaming herself?" Harlow whispers, paling. "I'd never—"

"We know," he tells her gently.

"Will this help Harlow's case?" Malik asks.

"They might overrule it. They are going through her rape kit that is on file. I do know the victim didn't go straight to the police, so DNA might not be conclusive. However, I am optimistic that forensics will be able to find something for us to use. I'll keep looking into it, but as I said before, Harlow is my client."

My mind wanders to Kayla and what she went through at the hands of Davis.

Is she the mysterious witness?

I can't believe it. Not because I thought Kayla would never take a stand, but because her mum is cruel and heinous. She'd never allow Kayla to come forward.

I desperately want it to be her though. She deserves justice. She deserves to see justice served to the lad who hurt her.

I miss her.

I shake my thoughts of Kayla away and go back to what he said before. "Won't the witness's clothes be useless if they're years old?" I ask, wondering how it works.

"She bagged them into a sealed plastic bag as soon as she got changed. If there is any DNA, it will be on them. However, it can take up to a week to find out."

"Which will still be in time for court, right?" Malik asks.

Mason kisses my temple and pulls me closer. I close my eyes, basking in his comfort.

"That's the other news I came to give you. There's been a change in dates. The witness will be testifying the day you were meant to, and you will be testifying the day after. If the court hearings go well, then the sentencing should be held not long after."

Joan clucks her tongue. "Why can't they just hurry the process up? It's been months since it happened, and the case is still ongoing."

"She's right," Harlow murmurs. "My nerves can't take any more, and now people are getting hurt because of it."

"I know this must be hard for you, Harlow, but we have to follow procedure. I'm sorry," he explains, before adding, "This will give them time to go through all the new information. This is a good thing. You want us in there knowing *all* the facts."

"Okay," she whispers, resting her head against Malik's shoulder.

She's worried. I can see it in her eyes. And I understand. If someone is targeting witnesses, then she's in danger too. She's the main one in his case right now, and he could go for her next.

He piles his papers back into his briefcase before sliding off the stool. "I'll leave you to it. If you have any further questions, please don't hesitate to call me. If anyone confronts you over the case other than me and your family, do not engage. Call the police immediately and keep me updated. Until then, I'll call if I have any updates."

"I'll see you out," Joan offers.

I'm surprised she has been so civil with him. Before, she hadn't spared his feelings when she mouthed off, telling him he could shove his degree up his arse. I guess the talk Mark promised Malik he would have with her, worked.

"You okay?" I ask, watching Harlow.

She shrugs, wiping under her eyes. "Honestly? I feel sick."

"Why?" Malik asks, frowning down at her.

She throws her hands up. "Because the first time he mentioned there being another witness, I felt nothing but relief. I felt hope for the first time that I wouldn't need to be standing up in that courtroom on my own. But then I remembered why I'm there. Why they will be there. And I feel sick to my stomach, Malik. I'm sick of it all. He's a monster."

"Babe," he murmurs, reaching for her.

She pushes him away, her tears streaking her face. "No. How can the judge sit there and not see a criminal? How can they not see who he truly is? He shouldn't be able to walk the streets again. *Ever*. I want this to be over, Malik. Over," she cries out.

Malik pulls her into his arms, letting her sob onto his shoulder. "He will never hurt you or anyone else ever again, baby," he tells her. "There's no way on this earth they'll find him innocent. As for feeling guilty, don't. You have nothing to feel guilty for. We'll get through this, Harlow; together."

Her legs buckle beneath her, and he supports her weight, holding her against his body. Tears gather in my own eyes. I hate that my best friend is so torn and broken.

Maverick and Max pale, taking us both in. "Fuck," Maverick groans, before dashing out of the room.

Max, however, grabs the chippy bag before trying to make his escape. I step away from Mason, blocking his way.

"I don't fucking think so," I snap.

"Denny," he whines, clutching the bag to his chest.

"No. I'm hungry. If you want to starve your niece then I'll happily remind her of that when she's older."

His lips part, and he inhales sharply. "That's blackmail!"

I arch an eyebrow and hold my hand out for the bag. "That's life. Now give it to me."

He grumpily passes it over, and I smile in triumph.

At least something went right today.

———

I t's getting late, and although I'm tired, I'm enjoying chilling on the sofa, catching up on some soaps and playing *Candy Crush*. *Coronation Street* is just ending when Max storms into the room, sweat trickling down his temples. He has been helping the others bring in my clothes and take them upstairs.

"You look comfy," he comments, a frown marring his forehead as he wipes the sweat away with his T-shirt. "Are you having fun?"

I don't care for his sarcasm, but it doesn't hurt to pay him back. I grin, stretching out further on the sofa. "Oh, I most certainly am."

He grunts, shaking his head in disgust. "You're lucky I don't want to be a part-time uncle, Denny, because otherwise, I'd be making you carry those goddamn clothes up yourself," he whines.

I laugh at his put-out expression. "I'm pregnant, you dipshit. We aren't supposed to lift anything heavy," I remind him. "What crawled up your arse?"

He grunts, which he seems to be doing a lot around me today. I'm not taking offence to it. It's Max. He's treating me like he would treat anyone else in his family—which can sometimes be annoying. But I'd hate it if he treated me differently. It wouldn't be the same.

"If you didn't have so many fucking clothes, I wouldn't be in this mood. Do you seriously need that many?" he asks, not letting me reply before continuing. "I mean, you do realise there are only seven days in a week, right? That's seven outfits, fourteen if you include spares. Not you. *Nooo*. You have to have an outfit for every day for the next three years."

I burst out laughing, unable to hold it in. "Max—"

"Max, get your fucking mangey arse out here and help with the shoe boxes," Malik snaps.

My stomach hurts when I begin to laugh harder. His expression is priceless and one I will never forget.

Before he can move, I quickly grab my phone, bring up the camera app, and snap a picture.

He glares at me, his features tightening. "I'll make you pay for this one day, Denny. I really will," he warns, before stomping out of the room.

I'm still laughing when Mason and Harlow stroll in, both looking exhausted. When they see me, both arch an eyebrow.

"What's got you so happy?" Mason questions.

"Yeah, I'd be careful, considering that bladder of yours," Harlow warns, and my laughter dies away.

Because she's right.

I pull my legs up, giving her room on the sofa, and hold my phone out. "Max. He came in moaning about all the boxes, and then Malik yelled for him to go help. It was hilarious."

Harlow pulls my phone away from me, laughing. "I've got to send that to my phone. Max and Myles' birthday is coming up soon. I am so going to put this in the paper."

Mason and I laugh at her excitement. It's nice to see her smiling again. She hasn't been right since the lawyer left, and I know she's still going over everything that was said.

My stomach grumbles loudly, and I groan. "I'm so hungry."

"Me too," Harlow moans.

"Me three," Mason adds, taking a seat in front of the fireplace.

"Me four, for whatever it is," Max snaps when he storms back into the room, his face red and sweaty once again.

"It's to clean up the garden so that Denny doesn't trip. We needed another helping hand," Harlow gushes, giving me a sly wink.

His face falls, and he pales. "Fuck! I just remembered I can't. It messes with my allergies. Sorry, peeps."

He doesn't look sorry as he takes a seat in the armchair, making me want to laugh.

"Well, thanks for your support, asshole," Mason growls.

"You didn't carry all those clothes, Mase. They were fucking heavy as shit. Did you see how many runs I did to get them all up the stairs? How the hell are you supposed to get them in that wardrobe? I know it's big, but, bro... those clothes need their own house."

"That's an over-exaggeration and you know it," I snap, taking offence.

"Babe…" Mason says, arching his eyebrow. "I'm the one who packed them into the van. There are tons and you know it."

I cross my arms over my chest, sniffing. "Sorry for wanting to dress nice," I tell him, before my shoulders sink into the sofa as I let out a sigh. "You'll probably have to get rid of most of them anyways. I probably won't fit into them after the baby is born."

Max shoots a glare at Mason. "If there are any more clothes, do not bother to call me. I'll be washing my hair."

My stomach grumbles again, demanding food. "What are we having for dinner then? I'll buy it this time."

Max leans forward, licking his lips. "Now you've mentioned it, I'm fucking starving."

"When aren't you?" Harlow teases.

"When I watch those programmes like, 'How Clean is Your House?'. They put me off food, if you can believe it. Oh, and at school. Whenever I think of the cafeteria food, I lose my appetite."

I playfully roll my eyes before turning to Mason, ready to ask where the others are. But Maverick and Myles take that moment to walk in with bags of Chinese takeout.

"We brought gifts." Maverick grins, holding the bags up. "Malik's just gone to get some plates."

"We were just about to order something too," Mason admits.

Maverick grunts. "We knew Denny and Max wouldn't last another twenty minutes without eating, so we called them half an hour ago and went to pick it up on our way back from the skip. You finished with the boxes?"

Mason tips his hand side to side. "Nearly. We just need to unpack the rest of Denny's clothes and shoes."

"The place does look homey now that everything is moved in," Maverick comments, taking in the room.

He's right. But there's one thing missing. "It just needs some pictures up and it will be a home."

"And a baby girl," Mason adds softly, his gaze on my stomach.

My heart melts at his words. When he meets my gaze, his eyes are warm. I smile, watching as he gets up from the floor.

"Any chance you could scoot up, babe?"

I grin sheepishly. "Sorry."

I scoot up, letting him sit between me and Harlow, just as Malik walks in. He frowns when he sees there isn't a seat next to Harlow, before parking his arse on the floor in front of her.

We only have a three-seater and an armchair. There isn't room for anyone else, but I have an idea about that. Once we're settled in, I'm going to buy beanbags. The others don't seem to care as they take up space on the floor, piling food onto their plates.

Myles kneels in front of the tele and scans through the DVD's piled on the floor in front of it. He pulls one out of the pile, grinning. "I love this film, *Nightmare on Elm Street.*"

"Can't we watch something else?" Max whines like a two-year-old.

"Nah, put that on," Mason orders, his eyes sparkling as he turns to me. "I wouldn't have pegged you as a horror film chick."

I arch an eyebrow. "They aren't horror movies, Mason," I tell him dryly.

"Yeah, it is. I fucking shit my pants and couldn't sleep for a week because of Freddy. I was scared he'd come for me," Mason admits.

Max starts slapping food onto his plate a little aggressively. "Don't even talk to me about horrors. I watched *Scream* once with a girl at the cinema. I wasn't paying attention to the movie at first because I was staring at the girl's tits. But then the tits on the screen distracted me and I began to watch it. *Big* fucking mistake. It was horrible. No girl with tits like that should be murdered first," he rambles, before reaching for another bag and grabbing food out of there. "It wouldn't have been so bad, but the girl I went with jumped in my lap, crushed my dick, then spent the rest of the movie screaming, 'I can't watch this', like a baby. It was the worst date ever." He pouts, his shoulders dropping. "I didn't even get to feel her up."

When we all burst out laughing, he huffs, grabs his food, and takes his seat, all while glaring at us all.

"Remember that time as a kid when we made him watch *Hocus Pocus?*" Maverick asks Mason, chuckling.

Max sits up, giving his brothers a warning look. "Shut the fuck up."

I rub my hands together. "This I have to hear. I love that movie, and I'm still shocked over you crying over *Scream*, because that has to be one of the funniest horror movies ever made."

Maverick hands me a plate of food before sitting back. "Our dad left us for the night. We never got the chance to watch the television, so we thought we'd make the best of it. There wasn't much of a choice back then, since we only had basic channels, but *Hocus Pocus* was on, and we decided to watch it. We weren't even halfway through the movie before he started screaming and crying. You know the zombie, Billy?" When we all nod, he continues. "When he rose out of the grave, Max got so scared he nearly pissed himself."

When Max glances at Mason, his frown turns into a smug grin. "I don't know why you're laughing; I can remember you crying like a baby while watching *Wrong Turn*," he taunts.

"My eyes were watering because I was laughing so hard," he replies dryly.

I turn my attention to him, my lips parting in shock. "You laughed?"

He frowns, nodding. "Yeah, why?"

"I laughed at that movie too," I tell him, liking that we have another thing in common. "You'd run the way you came, wouldn't you? You wouldn't run *into* the forest?"

"I know," Mason groans, his eyes wide. "And when they run into the abandoned shed, looking for a phone…" He rolls his eyes. "Stupid. Why would they even think there would be a phone in there? The place had campfires outside, for Heaven's sake."

"Don't get me started. It's like when they hide under the bed or they decide to find out what the *strange* noise is," I ramble, before snorting. "Not me. I'd lock myself up in my room until I heard something else, then I'd call the police."

"I wouldn't run," Max adds. "Fuck that. I refuse to spend my last moments running."

Harlow nods, agreeing. "Word."

I tune them out, my mind going to what I just said. I was in that nightmare. I did lock myself up and I did call the police. I don't want to put another downer on the day, so I force a smile for the others, grateful I have them in my life.

I just hope they'll still want me in their lives once Mason realises I'm not who he wants. No matter how much he tries, or what words he gives me, that fear is still there. It's unfair, and I know that, but the heartache he put me through, it was… catastrophic. I don't want to go through that again.

I know a part of that fear is because my feelings for him are no longer dormant. There's no longer a way for me to lock them up into a box and forget they exist. It's Mason. He's the love of my life.

Max points his finger at each of us. "Did you two seriously have some kind of freaky foreplay going on there? It's a horror movie, not a porno." He curls his lip up, unable to look at us.

I chuckle at his comment before turning to the television, getting engrossed in the movie.

By the time it's finished, and everyone has left, I'm knackered. Mason finishes straightening the pillows before turning to me. "You ready for bed?"

I yawn, nodding. "I am."

We head upstairs and enter the room we will be sharing. A nervous flutter erupts in my stomach. I've avoided thinking about this all day, but now that I'm staring at the bed, it's all I can think about.

We're going to be sharing a bed.

I'll be close to him, close enough to smell his earthy cologne. It's going to kill me.

He pulls back the bedsheet, looking up at me. "Um, so… How do you want to do this?"

My first thought is to reply, 'on my back'. After all, I know what it's like to be with him. But when he gets that devilish smirk, I chicken out. "What do you mean?"

He rubs a hand over his face. "The bed. Which side do you sleep on?"

"On this side," I answer, pointing to the side I'm standing by. I can't tell him I sleep in the middle. He'll probably learn that by himself soon enough.

He gives me a curt nod. "I'll go wash up."

After shutting the curtains, I get into bed, smiling as I take in the room once more. Out of all the rooms, this is my favourite. The walls are a deep purple, with black empty frames hung in places. On the main wall, the one behind the headboard, are three 3D butterflies.

I love how he's matched all the black furniture, including the ceiling fan that hangs in the middle of the ceiling.

The best feature has to be the reading nook in the window. The seat is long in length and depth. He's fitted a thick, plush seat, and has decorated the area with pillows of all sizes. What I love most is that the window is lower than the rest in the house, giving me a view of our shared garden. It will be amazing when it rains because I can listen to it whilst reading my favourite book.

It's my dream bedroom, and I know Harlow had a hand in it. She knew what I wanted after I showed her pictures one night when I slept at hers. The only thing missing is the four-poster bed with a white canopy that drapes down the sides.

It doesn't matter. I love it. But I love the trouble he went to, to make this our home, more.

Mason flicks off the main light when he finishes up in the bathroom, and the room glows with the dim light from the lamp. He slides into bed and flips off the lamp before pulling the covers over him.

I do the same and lie there, rigid, too afraid to move. I'm not sure why. We've been here before.

"Relax. I can feel how tense you are from here."

"I can't help it," I whisper, turning to face him.

He shoves his hand under his cheek, watching me. "Everything will be okay. I promise."

"That's not why I'm tense," I admit. "I'm scared this will end."

"It won't. I promise you. I never meant to hurt you the first time. I only wanted to protect you."

"I know," I admit, letting out a sigh.

"I'm being me, Denny. No more easy-going, uncaring, joking persona. I'm going to be me. And eventually, you'll see that," he explains. "Get some sleep. We have time to figure this out."

"Okay," I whisper, rolling back over to the other side, hoping he's right.

Because I desperately want this to work, and not just for the baby's sake.

But for ours.

CHAPTER
THIRTEEN

DENNY

A week of living alone with Mason—sleeping in the same bed and walking around in confined spaces with him—has been total and utter chaos on my mind. From the first night we shared a bed, I have slowly been losing my mind. I often wake up during the night, snuggled into his arms, my head resting in the nook of his neck.

Now... Everything he does is driving me wild. The way his lips close around a spoon, or the way he looks when he walks out of the shower wearing only a towel around his hips, showing his well-defined body, flashing the 'V' leading down to his groin. It's *everything* he does.

He's sending me stupid. I've even resorted to being a bumbling mess when I'm around him, always stuttering on my words. The once sassy, take-no-prisoners woman is long forgotten. It's like he's put me under some sort of spell, one where I can't have one lucid thought for myself.

He doesn't seem to be affected like me; but then, he also hasn't been the same person since I got back from Wales. The playboy I once knew is long gone, and in his place is a grown man making a living and acting sensible. The old Mason would have had me stripped down naked and thoroughly fucked by now.

He still flirts outrageously, yes, but it's more this time. He means every word. He's not using cheap pick-up lines.

It isn't just my desire to have him that's getting to me. It's been hard adjusting to our living arrangements. There have been times when I wanted to smack a pillow around his head. He's often left the toilet seat up—even though I stuck a post-it-note above the flusher, warning him to flush it and to put the seat back down. He leaves his clothes all over the bedroom floor too. And I've lost count of the amount of times he's walked through the house with dirty boots on.

I'm not the only one to have noticed a change in him though. Harlow mentioned the others have noticed too, but swore it's a good change. He's more relaxed, lighter, and he genuinely laughs like he means it.

When Maverick cornered me one day, he said the same thing. He's glad I'm here for Mason. For a long time, he was worried Mason was travelling down a dark road, one he would never come back from.

I disagree. That light in Mason has always been there for me. If he has changed, it isn't because of me. I think it might be because he's hiding something.

He has been acting differently, like the others said, but it's not just the way he acts or behaves. It's something more. And right now, it feels like he's keeping something from me. There have been a few occasions when I could have sworn he lied. It started the other day, when he came back soaking wet from the rain. I asked him where he had been, and he said work. But I know there's no way he got that soaked walking from his car to the house.

Then there's the phone calls. I tried to eavesdrop on a few occasions, but each time, I could never get close enough to hear or he'd end the call abruptly.

It only makes me more paranoid.

If he wants this to work—to really work—he has to be honest with me. I want him to want me the way I want him. Like I've always wanted him.

How can he claim I'm his, yet act this way? His secrecy, his hesitancy, it's blocking us from taking another step. It's stopping us from moving forward. We live together, we have a baby on the way, and there are affectionate touches here and there. But none of that means anything if we can't be honest with each other. Sometimes, I feel like we're just friends.

And I'm confused.

I'm horny, heavily pregnant, and the only one who can give me any kind of relief isn't making a move. He also isn't giving me a reason to make a move myself.

And slowly, I'm going insane.

Mason pulls me into his arms from behind, stopping me from grabbing my bag. He bends down, resting his chin on my shoulder. "Are you sure you have to go?"

I inwardly groan. This is why I need to get out. He's giving me mixed signals. "I need to get out for a bit," I tell him, pushing out of his arms and grabbing my bag.

When Harlow called and brought up going shopping, I jumped at the chance. I need some new maternity clothes and underwear that fit. With the additional weight, nothing is fitting me, and I'm running out of clothing options.

He blocks my path, reaching for my bag. "Is everything okay?" he asks, frowning down at me.

Sighing, I let it out all out, throwing my hands down at my sides. "Why don't you tell me."

"Huh? What are you going on about?"

His confusion only makes me angrier. He knows. He knows what this is doing to me. He must. Living under the same roof, the sleeping in the same bed; we're living like a family, but we aren't one.

And now he's keeping things from me.

If he has changed his mind about me, he needs to tell me now. I don't want to live here wondering if he's only with me for our daughter.

"You!" I yell, feeling my nose begin to sting. "You've been acting weird; keeping things from me and being secretive." I pause, catching my breath. "We're not really together, *together*. I know you said I wasn't ready. I know that. And I understand. But we live in the same house, Mason. I'm not blind. But what gives? What is going on with us?"

He walks calmly over to me, his expression blank. "Look, I'm going to come right out and say this before it goes too far."

He's going to ask me to leave. *I knew it.* Just like before, I can feel my heart crumbling.

"What goes too far?" I ask, pleading silently for him to go gentle with me.

He rubs the back of his neck, looking away, and I swallow past the lump in my throat. "The reason I haven't touched you is because you aren't ready. But neither am I. I'm making up for what I did, Denny. I truly am. But you left. You left without telling me you were pregnant," he starts. I open my mouth, ready to reply, when he continues. "This is killing me as much as it's killing you. *Trust me.* I want you so badly it hurts. But I'm still a man, Den. I have concerns just like you. And I'm fucking terrified that if I make another mistake, you'll leave again. I'm scared to death that you're only here because I forced you into it."

"I didn't know you felt that way," I tell him, my voice low. I hadn't expected him to say that.

"Now you do."

"You can't be serious though," I state.

"Deadly. I fucked up and I refuse to do it again. I don't want you to be ashamed of me or ashamed that I'm the father to our baby. I don't want you to be with me because I'm the father either."

"Mason, you have it all wrong. So very wrong," I tell him softly. "Do I want to do what's best for my child? Yes. I'll do anything to achieve that. What I wouldn't do is be with someone because society expects me to be with the father of my child. I had parents who were in a loveless marriage and look how that turned out." I take a breath, stepping closer. "And if you think I'd be here if I didn't really want to be, then you're wrong. I'm not ashamed of you in any way, shape or form."

"You truly want to be here? You aren't here just because of the baby?" he asks, hope filling his voice.

"God, no, Mason! I'm here with you because I want to be. I just feel like you don't feel the same way I do."

"Knew you couldn't resist me, babe." He grins playfully, grabbing me in his arms and swinging me around.

"I'll be sick," I warn, giggling.

"I don't care, babe. I've been stewing over this for far too long, but I didn't want to say anything because I'm selfish and didn't want you to leave me again," he explains, before continuing. "And I'll always want you."

I rest my hands over his chest, tears gathering in my eyes. "You really—"

"Cooeyyyy!" Nan screeches from somewhere outside. "*Oh my, aren't you a sight.*"

I groan. Hearing her flirtatious tone has me pushing out of Mason's arms and heading over to the front door. I pull it open, finding Nan and Myles out the front.

The other day, when Nan told Maverick she'd be here soon, he thought she meant that day. She didn't. She wanted to stop off at some friends' houses along the way.

"I'm really sorry, Miss, but this is private property," Myles warns her.

"Back in my day, they never made men like you. Such a shame too. You have such a fantastic body, young man," she tells him, eyeing him up and down like he's her next meal.

Myles' cheeks turn red, and he ducks his head, unable to reply. To save him from any more embarrassment, I step out, interrupting. "Nan, leave Myles alone."

Nan spins to face me, smiling wide. When Mason steps up beside me, she grins bigger.

Please no.

"You do pick well, my girl," she states, not once taking her eyes off

Mason. I can only be grateful he has on clothes. "I could have you for dessert."

I groan, slapping my forehead. "Seriously, Nan?"

"Alright, alright," she concedes, moving over to me. "Come give me some love. I've missed my favourite granddaughter."

"I'm your only granddaughter," I remind her.

"Yeah… well, it's the title that matters. Have you spoken to your father?" she asks, trying to seem unconcerned, but I know her. She's up to something.

"Nan," I warn.

She doesn't get it. Not really. She sides with me, but she doesn't understand how much it hurts. Dad hasn't bothered once to come and see me or contact me. If Mum doesn't want him to do something, he doesn't. Hell, I'm surprised he doesn't need her to tell him when to piss.

"Hear me out," she warns, not giving me a chance to say anything. "He's going to meet us today in town at a café. He wants to talk, and I think you should hear him out before we go shopping."

"Nan, I'm not talking to him. Please don't ruin this day for me," I plead, feeling Mason step closer. He pulls me against his chest for support.

"Shush, babe, hear her out," he whispers against my ear, before pressing a kiss just below. I sigh, distracted when Myles steps away and messes with the flowerbed, looking anywhere but at us. I roll my eyes. He's a Carter, so it's obvious he is going to listen.

Nan takes my hands in hers, squeezing gently. "He only wants five minutes of your time, honey. Please give him that," she pleads. If this was anyone other than my nan, I would just ignore them and tell them to fuck off. But it is Nan, and she's asking me to do something I'm not comfortable with. "I'll be dead soon. Give your nan one last wish."

"Are you freaking kidding me?" I squeal, throwing my hands up.

Harlow takes that moment to enter the garden, but stops when she hears my outburst, her eyes widening.

Nan inspects her nails. "Jesus… It's a joke, not a dick; don't take it so hard," Nan mutters. "I've got years in me."

I growl low in my throat as Mason struggles to keep his composure. It's only when Myles bursts out laughing that Mason lets it free, laughing uproariously.

"Mason," I growl. He isn't helping. Just as he stops, he starts up again.

Nan looks up from her nails, sighing. "Look, I know for certain that what your father has to say is something you'll want to hear."

"If you know then why don't you just tell me?"

"Where would the fun in that be?" she remarks, arching a brow. "Come on, he's waiting for us."

I groan, really not wanting to go now she's spoilt the day by bringing my father into it. I've been really looking forward to some girl time, and of course, getting some clothes that actually fit me. I turn in Mason's arms, blinking my lashes up at him, hoping he won't let her take me.

He grins and presses a kiss to my forehead. "Angel, he's your dad. If you don't feel comfortable and you want to leave, then just call me. I'll come and get you."

"You promise?" I pout.

"Always," he promises, kissing the tip of my nose. The action has me melting against him. "Now go on before your Nan strips the rest of Myles' clothes off."

When I turn to find her drooling and staring at Myles, I sigh. I walk over and click my fingers in front of her face, pulling her attention away. "Stop scaring him."

"I'd say I'm sorry, but I'm really not," she admits, grinning.

I roll my eyes. "Can we at least bring Harlow with us?"

"Of course," she answers. When I catch her sharing a look with Mason, I turn to find him giving her a quick nod.

"Is something going on?"

"No," Mason rushes out.

"Stop stalling," Nan demands.

Weirdos!

"Well, come on then. We haven't got all day," I snap, going back inside quickly to grab my bag.

———

Dad is sitting inside the café when we arrive, staring into his coffee mug. He hasn't seen us, so I take a minute to take him in. He's aged since I last saw him, which wasn't that long ago. His eyes hold a deep sadness that wasn't there before. And he looks exhausted, his cheeks hollow. Nothing like the well-presented dad I have known my whole life.

Nan trails inside before us, but I hold back a second, unsure of what I should do.

"Is he like your mum?" Harlow whispers, sounding genuinely scared.

He isn't. Not really. He just isn't the best dad.

I sigh, then open the door to the café and take a step in. "He's not, but sometimes his silence is worse," I admit, feeling deflated.

When he spots me, he stands, his eyes glistening with tears. "Denny," he chokes out.

When he pulls me in for a hug, I stiffen. It's the first time since I was five-years-old that he's shown me affection. It feels foreign to have his arms wrapped around me in such an affectionate embrace, like he feels like I'll disappear if he lets me go. It has me choking up, and my eyes begin to water. Then I remember all the years he's abandoned me, and I harden my stance.

"Dad, I need to breathe," I gasp out.

"Sorry. Yeah… You need air. I'm sorry," he stammers.

I arch an eyebrow, wondering where my dad has gone and what has happened for the sudden personality change. Because the man in front of me is a complete stranger.

"Why am I here, Dad?"

"Why don't we all take a seat," Nan announces. When no one makes a move, she gives me her 'don't push me' stare. I pull the chair out and take a seat.

He moves next, slower this time, unable to keep his eyes off me, like I'm a long-lost daughter and not the one he has practically neglected her whole life.

Harlow stands awkwardly at the edge of the table. "I'm going to, um, order a milkshake. Yeah, a milkshake. Does anyone else want anything while I go up there?"

I know she's doing it to give us some privacy, but I really don't want her to leave me alone with them right now. I grab her hand, looking at her with pleading eyes. She struggles for a moment, but my dad's next words relax her.

"They come over to take your orders," he explains. "And it's on me."

"Thank you, Mr. Smith."

"Call me Charles."

"Dad?" I call again, wanting him to say whatever it is he has to say so I can go and get me some trousers that stretch over my large frame.

"Yes, sorry, Denny."

He opens his mouth to continue, when the waitress walks over to take our orders. If I'm honest, I just want to strangle her and tell her to fuck off while my dad talks to me, but I'm not that sort of person. One thing my parents *did* teach me was manners.

As soon as she brings back our drinks, we all settle in to listen to my dad.

"How are you? And the baby?" he asks, his gaze softening on my large stomach.

What?

That can't be right. He didn't want me to keep the baby as much as my mother didn't want me to.

My lips twist into a snarl. "Why do you care? You made it perfectly clear where you stand, Dad."

"Denny, please listen," Nan snaps.

I whip my head around to face her, wondering why she's pushing me to listen to him when she told me she was on my side, that she didn't agree with what they had done to me. "He isn't saying anything."

"You're right, Denny," he starts before Nan can say anything else. "I've been a poor dad to you, and there are no excuses. None whatsoever. But I need to explain some things that happened before you were born."

"Go on," I tell him, trying to be firm but failing. I've spent my whole life wanting just this, and now that I've got it, I'm too angry with him.

Still, he is my dad, and it wasn't all bad.

"Before you were born, I was in love with a woman called Katie. We had been together for several years. One day, she broke up with me out of nowhere, and it devastated me to the point I went out every night to drown my sorrows. She left town shortly after. She never said goodbye or where she was going.

"It was then that me and your mother reacquainted. I was at a point in my life where I just wanted any kind of love—to feel loved. We had shared a brief affair many years before I met Katie, and we still ran in the same circles. I had hoped to mend my broken heart by being with someone. We dated for a few years, and I did start to care for her in my own way—even though everyone warned me she was pulling the wool over my eyes.

"One day, I started to see her in a different light. Before I could end our relationship, she told me she was pregnant with you," he explains, a wistful smile spreading across his face. "It was the happiest day of my life. I had always imagined having kids, so the second she told me, I wept with joy. I immediately asked her to marry me despite my concerns about her. Even my parents and friends warned me not to marry her. Still, I did it, wanting us to be a family. I thought having a child would change her. Change us.

"But she didn't change for the better. She changed for the worse. It was small things at first. Her tone changed, her beliefs changed; hell, even her views on others changed. Her outlook on people and life astonished me. She wasn't the same woman I first met. When you turned two, I knew there was no way out for me. It was a living hell. She admitted to getting pregnant for my family's wealth and connections." He pauses, a few tears falling down his cheeks. "Katie came back that year. She explained everything as to why she left. She told me how your mother and her group of friends ran her off by threatening her."

"Go on," I order softly, breaking inside. I've never seen him like this. Ever. And it's tearing me apart that I don't know what to do.

He nods, as if clearing a fog from his mind. "I told your mother I was leaving her, that I hated her for breaking me and Katie apart. Katie and I made plans to leave. She said there was one last thing I needed to know, but it was too big to tell and that I had to see. So I packed up our stuff, and we left. Me, you, and Katie. We were on our way to our new home when the car brakes stopped working," he explains, choking up.

"Oh my goodness," I breathe out, devastated for him.

Tears spill down my own cheeks. He did love me. There was a time when he put me first. He never left me with her; he took me.

"When I woke up in the hospital, your mum had taken over my care. I had just been told the love of my life had died, my daughter was injured but luckily okay, and I was depressed. I let it consume me. Guilt ate at me every time I looked at your mum. I kept thinking that maybe if I didn't leave her, Katie would still be alive. And I'd rather we had stayed miserable apart, because at least then, she would be alive.

"Your mother wasn't kind with her care. She let her anger show, and wasn't worried about the consequences."

"So why didn't you leave her once you were better?" I ask.

He looks up, his eyes solemn. "Because at the time, I believed your mother was responsible for cutting the brakes."

I sit up straighter, eyes wide. "What?"

"I tried to leave. I needed to go somewhere and grieve without her tormenting me. She said, 'Charles, don't be silly. Look what happened the last time you left me. You wouldn't want Denny to die next, would you?'. It was then that I realised I needed to stay. I was too scared to get on her bad side. I had to protect you."

I hold my hand up, unable to listen to any more. I need to process everything he said, but I can't. It's like there are a million voices screaming inside my head.

"Denny," he whispers.

I bang my fist on the table, rattling the drinks. "How could you? How could you let her treat me the way she did?"

He ducks his head. "I was scared of what she would do to you."

I wipe at the tears running down my face. "I'm eighteen, Dad. It's taken you eighteen years to tell me all of this? Why tell me at all? The damage has already been done. And you... *you* were just as bad. You ignored me."

"Stop," he demands when I grab my bag. "I had to, Denny. I really had to. Until you turned eighteen and could safely get out of her clutches, I had no choice. Whenever I paid attention to you as a kid, she would be cruel to you in so many ways. The further I pushed you away, the more she left you alone."

The getting locked in my room and the cupboard; the cutting off my hair; the torments... I remember it all. I remember the times she would be a bitch and I'd question her reasons for having kids at all. And there were times she ignored me completely. Those were a relief and a punishment, especially when she was kind to Evan.

And all this so she could have money.

"You're a coward," I snap, dropping my bag down on the floor.

"I've left her," he whispers. "I won't live without you in my life, Denny. I can't. I waited until I knew you were safe to file for divorce on the quiet. Then you came back, and at first, I got scared she'd get you to do her bidding. But then the day at the fair, I saw you'd never let her win ever again. I was a coward. I *am* a coward. But I know you're safe now. She can't threaten to disappear with you so I'll never get to see you again. She can't do anything."

It all feels so surreal. I've never painted my mum as anything but a bitch because that's what she is. But this... this is something else entirely. I never thought she'd stoop to this level.

My baby girl kicks at my stomach, and I grimace at the sharp pain. It reminds me of the gift I hold inside of me, and my eyes widen.

"Wait, are we safe from her?" If she did that to keep my dad with her, then she could do it again and hurt me and the baby in the process. Our lives are already at risk. We don't need to add another danger to the list.

His eyes soften a little as he nods. "Yes. She'll be leaving by the end of the month. There is nothing left for her here. I've taken everything. She signed an agreement. She can either throw a tantrum and get nothing, or she can leave quietly with the one-way ticket to the other side of the country and live in the new house I bought her."

"None of this feels real," I murmur, closing my eyes.

Harlow places her hand over my leg, gently squeezing. I give her a warm smile, although I'm breaking inside.

Nan scoots her chair forward, giving the side-eye to Dad. "It's true. What he's too scared to tell you is there's more to the story. When your dad came to me for help not long ago, I hired an investigator to look into things. Not only has your mum broken her prenup agreement by admitting on tape the real reason she was with your father, but our investigator also found some evidence that your mother caused the crash. It's not enough to get a conviction, but it was enough to get her to leave quietly."

"Why didn't you ever tell me?" I whisper, feeling betrayed that she knew.

She places her hand over mine. "I wanted you to know it all at once. I was never going to keep it a secret, sweet girl."

I glance at Dad, wondering if this can really work between us. Can we mend what is broken? I don't know, but I want to find out.

"So all the times you agreed with her, it was because you didn't want her to hurt me?"

"Of course," he rushes out, sincerity in his voice.

"You didn't mean it then, when you told me to get rid of the baby?"

There's sadness lurking in his gaze, but I can't deny there is happiness there too. "I may have seemed distant from your life, my girl, but I was always paying attention. Always. When you told me you were pregnant, I was ecstatic about becoming a grandfather, but I knew if I showed it, she would do something to make you lose the baby."

"You said I ruined my life, that I'd never get a respectable job."

He smiles. "You can rule the world, my girl, and do it with a dozen babies. I never, for one second, thought being pregnant would stop you from chasing your dreams."

"Really?" I ask, feeling my throat tighten.

This is all I ever wanted. His approval. His love.

She took so much from me, and I hate her for it.

"Really," he agrees, a small smile playing on his lips. "If it's okay with you, can I meet Mason, the father?"

"Yes," I agree, feeling giddy inside.

"Speaking of, we should get back," Harlow announces, frowning.

"What? Why? We just got here."

"We've been here nearly two hours," Harlow reveals, laughing when my jaw drops. "Malik texted and said to get our arses back. He needs to speak to us."

I look at her warily when she doesn't meet my gaze. When she doesn't give in, I sigh. If we ignore him, he'll only come looking for her anyway. Malik hates it when she does.

"Why don't you come with us, Charles?" Nan asks, gathering her things.

"I wouldn't want to intrude."

"No, come. Mason would love to meet you," I lie. I don't know how Mason is going to react to all of this. When we collected my belongings, he never stopped glaring at my dad, cursing under his breath every two minutes.

"I doubt that," he adds, chuckling. "But I'd love to."

I came here thinking the worst, but Nan was right. I did want to hear this. As heart-breaking as this has been, I want to start fixing what she broke.

And this is a start.

FOURTEEN

DENNY

When we get back, I'm surprised to find it eerily quiet. There's always one or more Carter's hanging around, but right now, there isn't a soul in sight.

Turning to Harlow, I arch an eyebrow. "I thought you said they were here?"

She scans the garden, not meeting my gaze. "That's what they said."

What isn't she telling me?

Anxiety swarms in my stomach. My steps are rushed as I head to the house, pulling my key out of my pocket. I push open the door, my heart racing.

If it's something to do with Mason, I want to know.

"Surprise!" is yelled as I step through the doorway.

I gape at everyone standing in our living room. Mark, Joan, and the rest of the Carter brothers are here. Joan has even brought Edna, her friend.

Banners with 'It's a Girl' are pinned up on the walls, along with 'Welcome to Your New Home'. Different shades of pink balloons are scattered around the room, some with 'baby girl' written on them.

I hold my hand to my chest, rubbing the ache there. This is too much.

Mason steps away from the crowd, a grin spreading over his face. I'm speechless. Did he do this?

His grin slips into a fierce frown. "What?" I ask.

"What is he doing here?" he grits out, glancing over my shoulder. "I thought you were just talking."

Shit.

I walk over to him and place my hands over his chest. "Calm down." When he doesn't, I wrap my arms around his neck, pulling him down until we're eye level. "It's a long story, one I'll tell you, but for right now, trust me. Please," I plead.

"But he—"

"Trust me," I repeat. "Just give him a chance."

He watches me closely before giving me a firm nod. "Okay. For you, I'll try."

"Thank you," I breathe out, then take a look at the room once more, smiling. "Was this the secret? The thing you've been whispering about on the phone?"

He grins, pulling me closer against him. "I told you: I'll always be honest—just not when it comes to surprises." He kisses my forehead before pulling back. "Do you like it?"

"I love it," I admit.

I feel a presence behind me, and Mason tenses. He glances down at me, resting his forehead against mine. "If he hurts you, I swear to you, I'll hurt him back," he warns. "But I'll try. For you."

"It's all I ask," I whisper, leaning up to give him a peck on his cheek. I pull back, smiling at Dad. "Dad, this is Mason; Mason, this is my dad, Charles."

Dad holds his hand out. "It's good to meet you."

Reluctantly, Mason takes it. "You too."

The tension in the air relaxes once Mason gives his okay. The rest follow, introducing themselves to him.

I walk over to Myles when I see him eyeing up the food. "Where's Max?"

"He should be here any minute. I don't see why we have to wait to open the food until he gets here," he whines.

I chuckle, taking in the massive spread. They really went all out. But I can see what he means. I want to forget manners and help myself too. It looks so good.

The door opens as my fingers reach for the foil covering a plate, and the entire room erupts into cheers.

Max grins and bows dramatically, before heading over to me and Myles. "Did you miss me?"

"Brownies?" I question, curling my lip when I see the mess on the plate. There isn't any chocolate icing, and they have a weird colour inside them.

"No touching. We had to use raw egg, or it has some other ingredient that pregnant women can't touch, so fingers off," he warns. "I mean it."

I roll my eyes. He's just worried I'll have more than him. I'm tempted to eat them to spite him, but they really do look disgusting. "Your brownies are safe."

Joan begins to unwrap the food, and my stomach grumbles. I grab a plate and pile on some food before making my way through the house, back to Mason. He's sitting on the sofa with his granddad. When Mark spots me, he vacates the seat.

"No, it's fine. You can stay there," I tell him, hating that I've interrupted their conversation.

"Sit down, Denny," Mason orders. I shake my head in defiance.

"It's okay, I'm going to get some of that lovely quiche before it's all eaten," Mark assures me, giving Mason's shoulder a squeeze before exiting the room.

"Did you leave anything for the rest of us?" Mason questions, amusement in his voice when he takes in my plate.

I snort and sit next to him. "Yes, but this is for you too. I didn't want you to go without, so I piled everything on my plate."

"I knew there was a reason I… wanted you," he explains, smirking.

"Yeah, yeah," I retort, ducking my head so he can't see the smile spreading across my face.

My heart is beating rapidly. I know what he was going to say. Why he didn't say it, I don't know, but he can't undo that momentary pause.

"We're opening presents later. First, I want to show you your surprise."

"My surprise?" I ask, my nose twitching.

"Yeah, your surprise. Well… It's for both of us. Kind of."

"Oh God, you didn't get a box of condoms, did you? I think it's a little late for that," I tease, letting out a giggle when his face reddens.

"No. Something much more needed," he explains, bumping his shoulder against mine. "Plus, we won't be using protection. I plan on getting you knocked up in another couple of years," he reveals, causing me to pause midchew and nearly choke on my food. "I'm joking, Denny. Breathe."

"Not nice," I snap, snatching the ham sandwich out of his hand.

This mama bear is hungry.

Once everyone is done eating, Mason stands, reaching for my hand. "Come see your surprise," he orders gently.

I nod and follow him up the stairs, the others following behind. I give him a 'what?' look, wondering what could be up here that he can't bring downstairs.

"Is this where things start to get kinky?" Joan whispers loudly.

"Grams, please shush, and stop talking dirty," Harlow pleads, making us all chuckle.

"I like it one-on-one myself," Nan adds.

I pause on the stairs, stopping to turn to Nan. "Nan, please take Harlow's incredible advice and shush it."

"Sheesh, lighten up. It was a joke."

I roll my eyes and continue up the stairs to where Mason stands outside one of the spare bedrooms, a grin on his face.

"What's in there?" I ask, wondering why he looks so jittery.

He holds his hands up. "Don't get mad. If you don't like anything inside, we can change it. I just wanted to do this for you, okay?"

His anxiousness is setting off my nerves, so all I can do is nod. The door creaks as he pushes it open.

The breath is stolen from my lungs as I step inside. The room is no longer piled with boxes, and gone are the plain, plastered walls. Now, three walls are painted a rose gold colour whilst the fourth is a light grey, decorated with different shades of pink butterflies. The carpet is a light shade of grey too, but with a rose gold rug that has 'I Love You to the Moon and Back' in white italic writing.

I step further into the room, walking over to the princess cot that takes pride of place against the grey wall. White netting drapes down and over the cot. Tears gather in my eyes. It won't be long until my daughter will be lying upon those butterfly blankets. It's a dream, and I can't wait for it to be reality.

I glance closer at the butterflies lining the walls, wondering why something feels different. I think it's because the butterflies are set like something should be in the middle.

Seeing where I'm looking, Mason steps closer. "I've left the space blank. We can put her name in wooden lettering there."

I ignore the others, who are silent in the room, and walk over to the chest of drawers, sliding my fingers over the white wood. Above it, Mason has decorated it with teddy bears. On the other side of the room is a bookshelf lined with various fairy tales fit for a princess. The place is absolutely magical.

Sat by the window is a white rocking chair. On one side of the adorable rocking chair is a mini table, and on the other is a changing mat table. The way Mason has it set up makes it look like the most comfortable place to relax. I twirl around in the middle of the room, feeling completely overwhelmed, until I lay my eyes upon Mason.

He's still standing by the cot, looking unsure of himself as he patiently waits for my reaction. I take quick strides over to him and wrap my arms around his neck. His warmth surrounds me like a blanket. I can't help but hold on tighter.

"Thank you so much," I tell him, feeling my throat close.

"So you like it?" he whispers against my neck.

"I love it, Mason," I tell him, pulling back. "It's perfect. You're perfect. Our girl is going to love this," I tell him honestly, not realising what I said until it left my mouth.

"You think I'm perfect?" he asks, his lips twitching.

I punch him in the arm, rolling my eyes when he rubs the spot like I actually hurt him. "Slip of the tongue," I tease.

"Yeah, I'd believe you, but your eyes tell me different," he tells me, his voice low and husky.

His pupils dilate and he steps closer, but then chaos erupts in the room. Nan begins to gush over the room, and everyone else follows suit, until Mason yells at them to get off the carpet if they're wearing shoes.

His tight expression has me giggling into the back of my hand, which only earns me a glare from him.

His expression softens somewhat. "I'll do anything to keep that smile on your face. Even if it means I have to redecorate our daughter's bedroom again and again," he admits.

He's serious.

"Mason—"

He steps forward and pulls me in for a kiss. I moan into his mouth, clinging to his shirt. Just as the kiss gets hotter, more frantic, Mason pulls away, panting for breath.

When I see we're now alone in the room, I arch an eyebrow at him, hoping he didn't regret it. "Why did you stop?"

His gaze darkens and he drops his forehead against mine, taking a deep breath. "I'm going to kill Max."

Max?

"What does this have to do with Max?"

He sighs, kissing me briefly on the lips. "Everyone left because he told them to. Apparently, getting a boner while watching your brother snog his woman is awkward as hell."

"He didn't?" I question, trying not to laugh and failing. I'm used to Max and his shenanigans, but still… I'm never going to live this down.

"He said, and I quote, 'Well, I don't know about you guys, but getting a boner while watching your brother snog some hot chick is uncomfortable as hell. Why don't we go before they start taking their clothes off and it goes beyond awkward?'"

I shove my face into his chest, my shoulders shaking with laughter. A few seconds later, he begins to laugh too.

"We should go back downstairs before they think we're actually doing it," I tell him.

He groans, but gives in. "Come on."

Chaos echoes up the stairs as we make our way down. When we reach the front room, everyone is circled around Joan and my nan.

I gasp when Joan pokes Nan in the chest. "I saw you eyeing up my man," Joan snaps.

"Oh, please, I was not eyeing him up. Why would I in a room full of hot, young beefcakes?" Nan retorts, smirking.

I groan and step forward to intervene, but Mason pulls me back against his chest.

"Like you stand a chance, you hu—"

"That's enough now, ladies. Let's enjoy the party and not fight over worthless men," Charlie, our friend from school, says from her spot on the sofa.

When did she arrive?

When Charlie started back at school after having so long off, Harlow and I began to hang out with her. She explained missing pieces when it came to Davis, since she was also best friends with Kayla Martins, a girl Davis assaulted.

"Charlie, sweetie, she keeps eyeing my man. If it's not my man then it's one of his boys," Joan explains, before her eyes scrunch together, flicking between Mark and Nan. She stomps over to Mark and slaps his shoulder. "Did you just wink at her?"

Mark's eyes widen. "What? No! Of course not."

"You did," Nan taunts, winking back at him.

He groans, dropping down into the chair, giving anyone who looks his way a helpless look.

"You're such a coward," Joan yells at him. "What, you can't handle me in the bedroom anymore, so you need someone tamer?"

There isn't a person in the room who doesn't groan. I'm pretty sure Max has just been sick in his mouth, if his expression is anything to go by.

"Honey, this isn't the time nor the place to talk about this," Mark soothes. "Can we all calm down?"

Joan cocks her hip. "So, you're not looking at her?"

"I only have eyes for you," he tells her, clutching her hands in his.

"Why do you only have eyes for me?" she rushes out, her gaze darting around the room. "Why couldn't you bring me chocolate and wine, like any normal person? Why eyes?"

"Romance is dead," Nan remarks.

"You'd think they'd use their initiative. In our day, we never had Doodle. We only had our brains. But even with technology, today's men still don't get it," Joan adds.

"It's *Google,* honey," Nan corrects. "I disagree. Google is like a woman. We have all the answers."

"You saying I'm thick?" Joan asks, and I mentally slap myself for not warning anyone about my nan beforehand.

"I feel like dancing. Who wants to dance?" Charlie yells, fist-pumping the air, before another fight can break out.

"What is wrong with them?" I whisper, eyes wide.

"Ohhhh, I love a good dance," Nan replies at the same time Joan says, "Let's shake what our mamas gave us."

She starts twirling her arse in a seductive hip curl, which I thought would be impossible given her age, but no, Joan has it covered perfectly.

"Is anyone else wishing her mother taught her the whole 'shake what ya mama gave ya' bullshit expires at the age of thirty?" Myles whispers. Max grunts in agreement.

"Oh, oh, I know. Charlie, you can teach us how to twirl." Nan claps excitedly.

"Who gave them the loopy juice?" I whisper to Mason, ignoring Myles' comment, otherwise I'll laugh and draw attention to myself.

"Fuck knows," he replies, chuckling. "But I'm going to need to bleach my eyes out after this."

"You and me both," I tell him, frowning at Charlie when she starts twirling.

"That's not twirling," Nan scolds. "That girl doesn't do it like that.

You know the one... she humps a wrecking ball."

"Oh, you mean twerking," Charlie states.

Nan waves her off. "That's what I said."

"I'm never going to unsee this. I'm never going to be able to look either of them in the eye again. What happened to grandmas staying at home, watching black and white movies whilst knitting and making us tea and biscuits?" Max whines, covering his face. "No, now we have to suffer through... through... I don't even know *what* to call this," he cries.

"I hear you, brother." Mason winces when Joan bends over, following Charlie's instructions, and starts shaking her butt.

"Hey, Denny, can I talk to you for a moment?" Dad asks, stepping up to us. He avoids looking in Nan's direction and I don't blame him.

"Sure. Is everything okay?" I ask, as Mason tenses behind me.

When the noise gets louder, I turn to Dad. "Let's go into the kitchen."

He nods and follows us out of the room. I kind of feel bad I haven't paid more attention to him. I pretty much left him to fend for himself with a group of crazies.

Honestly, if tomorrow's headlines don't read: Two Women are Wanted for Questioning... then I'll be shocked.

"What's up?" I ask once we're all inside the kitchen.

"I need to get going. The estate agent called when you were upstairs."

"Estate agent? You're selling the house? Why? Where are you going to go? Why would you make up with me then leave me? I don't understand," I tell him, my knees locking together.

How could he do this to me?

Mason supports my waist, pulling me against him. "I think you should go," Mason demands, his voice hard. A shiver races down my spine at the unspoken threat.

"You've got it wrong, baby girl. I promise. I'm selling the house, but I'm not moving away," he rushes out, pleading with me to believe him.

I do. I can see the fear of losing me again in his gaze. I shake my thoughts away, wishing I wasn't so hormonal lately.

"You aren't?" I whisper.

"I'm not," he promises, his gaze softening. "I hate that house. Who needs an eight-bedroom house when you'll be the only one occupying it? We never needed that much space to begin with. There was only four of us."

"What will you do?" I ask.

"I'm going to buy one closer to town, and a lot smaller. Maybe a two or a three-bedroom house. Maybe we can make up the spare bedroom just for the baby," he adds, his tone hopeful.

"Dad, that sounds amazing. We'd love it," I tell him, then look to Mason. "Wouldn't we?"

"Yeah," he grouches, forcing a smile.

"I'll be off then, but if you are free, we can do dinner in the week or something," he offers, rubbing the back of his neck.

"I'd love that," I admit, then rush out, "If you are free from work, that is."

He bends down, kissing my cheek. "I'll always be free for you."

I can't lose him again. Not now I've finally got the dad I always wanted. I believe everything he said to me, although I'm still kind of processing. It hasn't all sunk in yet, and I have a feeling in my gut that I'm missing something.

Feeling his hesitation, I pull him in for a hug and squeeze him tightly. I don't want to let go. "Dad," I whisper, my nose stinging.

"I'm not going anywhere. I swear to you. I'm so grateful you're giving me a chance," he chokes out. When he pulls back, tears are glistening in his eyes. "See you soon."

I watch as he leaves and fall into Mason's arms. "I have so much to tell you."

"You can tell—"

The kitchen door flies open, and I jump when Nan tumbles in, her face pale and her eyes red-rimmed.

"Nan, what is going on?"

"Are you in labour? *Are you*? Have you eaten?" she rambles, before her pupils go cross-eyed. "Did I see you eat anything?" She cackles to herself, mumbling under her breath.

"What are you going on about?" I ask. I didn't see any alcohol anywhere, so she isn't drunk.

Mason tenses behind me. "Fuck me!"

"Did that, and it got me pregnant," I mutter dryly, before turning back to Nan. "Nan, why are you acting crazier than normal?"

"I'm fine. I'm not crazy, but that Joan woman is. Did you see the way she kept eyeing me? It's making me nervous and jittery. Oh, maybe that's her plan. She wants to get me at my lowest so she can catch me off guard when she strikes."

"Who's striking who?" Max asks, strutting in and taking a seat at the breakfast bar.

"He's another too," Nan whispers, her eyes narrowing on Max.

Max groans, lifting his head out of his hands. "Another what, Mary?"

"Another one who can't stop staring at me. It's going to blow my chances with Myles," she explains, dead serious.

I splutter whilst Mason collapses against the counter, laughing. Max, on the other hand, pales. "I'm the better fucking twin," he argues.

The noise must gain attention from the others because first, Joan walks in, then Mark, then Myles and Charlie. I can't see Harlow or Malik anywhere.

Nan spots Myles, and her eyes nearly burst from their sockets. 'Hey, handsome. How about that dance now?" she asks, seductively walking over to him.

He pushes her roaming hands off him. "What on earth is going on with them?"

When Joan starts laughing for no reason, I have to question it myself. "Seriously, what is going on with them? It's like they're drugged."

Max grabs a packet of crisps out of the cupboard before muttering, "They aren't drugged..." His eyes widen. "Unless they ate the brownies."

"Brownies?" Mason growls, and I put a calming hand on his arm. His breathing is shallow. I wonder what has him so worked up. "What. Did. You. Do?"

Max points to himself. "Me? Why do you always assume it's me? I'm not the bad twin, you know. Myles has his share of bad. Just last night he robbed the last Snickers bar out of Maverick's stash."

"You fucker. I knew it was you," Maverick growls, glaring at Myles. He turns away, glancing over at me and Mason. "I'm off to work. Thanks for the… lovely evening. Bye."

"Fuck you, Max. You're the one who set the bedsheets on fire when you tried to set your fart on fire, so don't bring me into this," Myles huffs, before following Maverick out the door.

"Great," Mason barks. "You're running all our guests away."

He isn't wrong. One by one, people are leaving. Only me, Charlie, Max, Mason, Nan, Joan and Mark remain in the house.

"I'm pretty sure that was Joan and Mary when they offered to show us men what a real strip tease was," Max snaps, affronted.

My mouth gapes open when I turn to Nan and Joan. Neither look the least bit embarrassed, nor do they even try to deny it. In fact, they're acting as if Max just told the funniest joke on earth.

I glare at Max. They're stoned.

Oh my god, they are stoned.

"Max, I'm going to wring your fucking neck," I snap, stomping over to him.

He slides over the breakfast bar, his face pale. "What did I do?" he yells, dodging me once again. "Mason, stop her."

"You got them stoned with your fucking brownies," I growl, then decide he deserves a little payback. I make my bottom lip tremble. "Max, my nan has a heart defect. If it slows down to a certain rate, she can go into shock, collapse, and then die. Nothing will be able to save her."

It could be true. It could have repercussions. And then there's the fact this is a baby shower.

What if I had eaten one?

He pales, running over to Nan. "Fuck! You need to dance to get your heartrate up," he yells, grabbing her hands. He begins to dance with her, treating her as if she's a rag doll, waving her arms around.

I let him believe the lie a moment longer, enjoying his discomfort.

It's only when Nan turns a little green that I begin to worry. I place my hand over my mouth when she throws up... all over Max's white shirt.

"Why does it look like there are carrots in that vomit? We didn't have carrots," Mason grumbles, before gagging.

The harsh stench has me wanting to vomit too.

"Oh my God, she's foaming from the mouth. Someone h-help... Fucking hell, that stinks," Max squeaks, turning to retch over the kitchen sink.

He quickly pulls his shirt off, and I ogle his fine physique, before Mason grunts. I shrug, smiling. I'm still a woman, and for a seventeen-year-old, Max does have quite the package. It's just a shame he opens his mouth.

And he isn't Mason.

"I think I'm going to be sick," Joan moans. Mark takes her hand and steers her towards the door. "I've got sick on me. It's all over me, Mark. Get it off! Get it off!"

Her voice fades out, and I turn to Nan to make sure she's okay. She is, though she's swaying in the chair Charlie pulled out for her.

I glare at Max. "You!" When he looks up, he pales. "You can take Nan back home. I can't believe you'd do something this stupid. What if they had a bad reaction or I had eaten them?"

He grabs one of Mason's clean shirts from the ironing pile and shoves it over his head. "I told you not to touch them."

"Oh my god," I snap, throwing my hands up. "Do you not realise telling someone they can't have something only makes them want it more? You're so fucking lucky I was craving red onion and not them, because I would have eaten the entire batch."

"Denny—" he starts.

I hold my hand up, turning to Mason. "Get him out of my sight before I kill him," I demand lightly, before stomping upstairs.

When I get to the top, I don't go into our room. Instead, I turn left and head back into the nursey, a smile on my face.

CHAPTER
FIFTEEN

DENNY

I throw the remote onto the end of the sofa with a groan. I'm bored, sexually frustrated, and struggling with seriously bad heartburn. I didn't even realise a pain like this could exist. It's all getting to me, and I'm ready to explode.

Mason must have sensed it because he declared he was taking me out again tonight on another date. We haven't had a chance to do much together since he's usually either working or I'm asleep. When we have, we've watched a movie and had some kind of takeout.

I need a change of scenery.

There's a knock on the door, and I nearly roll to the floor in my bid to get off the sofa. Once I straighten myself, I head over to the door.

I know it's Harlow. She wants to go to court with just her grandma and Malik, in case anyone is hanging out outside the courtroom again. And because our shopping trip was cut short, I promised we could do it after court to keep her mind off things.

When I pull open the door, I'm greeted by Harlow, who looks

worse for wear. "Hey, what's happened?" I ask. Then I notice the flowers. "Why do you have lilies?"

She shakes her head. "They were left by your door."

My forehead creases into a frown. "They must be from Mason. We've got a date tonight."

Tucking her hair behind her ear, she bites her lip. "Aren't lilies meant for funerals?"

Shit! I twirl the flowers in my hand, picking up the card taped to the side. "Yes, they are." I gesture for Harlow to follow me and place the flowers down on the counter.

When I pull the note out of the envelope, I inhale sharply.

What the hell!

"What's wrong?" Harlow asks, stepping closer.

My hands shake as I hold up the note. "It says *'Now may you rest in peace.'* How creepy is that?"

"I don't think Mason sent those," she tells me, her voice quivering.

I agree, which is why I pick up my phone and call him. It doesn't ring for long before he answers.

"Aww, babe, are you missing my sweet arse already?"

My lips twitch into a smirk, forgetting about the note for a second. "Yes, because I can't go more than four hours."

"True. I barely got a goodbye out of you when I left four hours ago," he reminds me, chuckling. "What's up?"

"Oh, um, by any chance did you buy me creepy lilies?" I ask.

"Uh, no. I'd do better than lilies. Why? Did you get some?"

"I did."

"I swear, if it's Max or Myles playing a practical joke, I'll knock 'em out," he growls.

"Well, if they wanted to freak me out, it's worked," I admit, my chuckle dry.

He's silent for a moment, before he quietly asks, "What do you mean?"

"There was a note. It says, *'Now may you rest in peace.'*"

"What the fuck?" he growls. "Do you know where they're from? I'll call up the company."

"Hold on," I tell him, tucking the phone to my ear and shoulder as I turn the card over. No name or company details are located on the card, so I check the flowers, but see nothing on them either. "No, nothing."

"I'm coming home," he declares.

Relief fills me, but then I glance over at Harlow, who looks lost in thought. She hasn't said anything, but I know she needs me right now.

"No, stay there. It's fine. We can talk about it later. Harlow's here," I explain, hoping he can hear my hidden meaning.

"All right. Everything okay?"

"I'll let you know."

"Let me know if you want picking up from town. I'll be finishing after three," he offers.

"Okay. Speak to you later," I tell him, before ending the call.

"Why don't we sit down and talk," I offer. She nods, her shoulders slumped as she makes her way into the front room.

Once we're seated, I begin. "What happened today?"

She fiddles with the rip in her jeans, her lip trembling. "The final hearing is in two weeks. You should have seen him, Denny. He looked right at me. There was so much hatred, I could feel it in my soul," she whispers, her body shivering.

I wrap my arm around her shoulders. "He can't hurt you anymore."

"What if they don't believe me? What if they set him free? He's making up lies that sound so believable, even I'm questioning myself, and I know what went down that day," she babbles, before tears slip free. "He was going to rape me. How can they let him go free?"

"Harlow," I whisper, wiping her tears away.

She shakes away my touch, getting up. She paces in front of me. "He'll do it again if he gets free. He'll come after me. What will it take for them to see what a monster he is? Does he need to rape me to be convicted? Today, they basically said no crime was committed because he didn't touch me. What if he gets out and succeeds in raping me next time?"

I stand and place my hands on her shoulders to stop her from pacing the floor. "Harlow, you need to calm down."

"I can't, Denny. My chest feels so tight," she breathes out, clutching her chest. "I thought I was coping with everything, that I was moving on from what he did, but I'm not. I'm still stuck in that mouldy-smelling bedroom, feeling the hard bedsprings in my back and feeling petrified. I can't go back there. I can't. I won't."

"Hey," I snap, shaking her. She blinks up at me, tears spilling down her cheeks. "You *can* do this. You *are* doing it. He hasn't got the power to take that away from you, Harlow. You're strong, you're beautiful, you're independent, and you've overcome much worse, babe. Don't let him win. Don't let him have the pleasure of knowing he's gotten to you, or that you're scared. Because I know you are.

"When I woke up on the ground that night, the first thought I had was you. I remember feeling powerless to help you. I was so scared. He'd already put you through enough. But Harlow, if anyone can get through this… it's you. You're the strongest person I know."

"I can't, Denny. I just can't. His face today…" she sobs out, shivering. "It was a promise of retribution. I just wanted to run out of that courtroom. The way his lawyers ripped into me, talking about a sordid relationship that we never had. I felt dirty and ashamed. It's why I needed to have a hot shower before I came over. He makes me feel like that every night in my nightmares," she explains.

Tears fill my own eyes as I pull her in for a hug, clinging to her. Her pain feels like my own. I hold her tightly, hoping to give her some comfort.

"Have you spoken to Malik about any of this?"

"No, and you can't tell him about what I told you. I don't want him to think that I'm weak. I'm just so fucking scared," she admits, pulling away.

I wipe back the hair that clings to her wet cheeks. "You need to talk to him before this consumes you. You've got me. You always have. But Malik gives you something I can't. Let him help you. You're strong, remember that. Don't cling to the fear; focus on your future happiness, because that's all that matters. Davis isn't going anywhere other than Hell."

"Grr, I'm being so silly," she groans, wiping her tears away.

"No, you're not; you're being human."

"I'm just scared," she whispers.

"You wouldn't be human if you weren't," I point out.

"Urgh, look at me. I look a mess and we need to go if we want to get you an outfit."

"We can stay here if you prefer. I've got loads of clothes, so we can stay in and watch a movie instead." I smile, hoping she confides in Malik later on. Because although I'll always be here for her, I meant what I said earlier. He can give her something I can't; and heal her in a way I won't be able to.

She waves me off. "No. No. It's fine. I'll just go sort myself out, then we'll go."

"Are you sure? I honestly do not mind," I tell her, truly not wanting her to do something she's not up for.

"Honestly, it might do me some good to get out and take my mind off things."

"All right, you go and sort yourself out whilst I dispose of those flowers."

I walk into the kitchen to throw the flowers into the bin. Once I hear the bathroom door close upstairs, I pull my phone out of my pocket and message Malik.

Me: She isn't taking the court case as well as we thought. D x

Malik: I'm coming over.

Fuck! He can't come over. She'll know then that I just tattled on her, even if this is for her own good. She needs help, but she also needs to know she's strong enough on her own.

Me: No!!!

Me: We're having a girl's day. Don't ruin it. D x

Malik: I'm not going to sit at fucking home while she's suffering, Den. She needs me.

Me: No, what she needs is a distraction. She needs her mind taken off what she went through, and going to town will help with that. I didn't text you so you'd go all caveman. I texted you to tell you that when she's back, be gentle with her. Get her to open up. Don't be an arse. Dx

Malik: Nice to have you back, Denny.

A grin spreads across my face. It does feel good to be back. I'm finally starting to feel like myself again, and not this self-conscious, insecure shell of a woman I'd become. I'm back to my old outgoing, bossy self. Nearly. I've still got a way to go before I'll ever feel normal again, but for the first time in a long time, I feel like it could happen.

———

Walking down Main Street, the wind picks up, and goose bumps break out over my skin. With the end of August approaching, I'm not at all surprised. British weather has never stuck to course.

Shopping isn't going as good as I had hoped. In fact, all it has done is put me in a bad mood. The woman in the last store literally followed us around the shop like we were common thieves. Then to top that off, she kept eyeing my bump like it was infectious. I wanted to claw her face with my nails.

"Okay, where to now, because that woman in the last store really needed to pop her eyes back into her head. Did you see the way she was staring at my bump?"

"Yeah, I did. For a second, I got worried you were going to go Michael Myers on her arse."

"Trust me, if I had a butcher knife, I would have used it on the bitch," I joke.

Harlow laughs. "Shit, you sound scary. Remind me never to get on your bad side."

I'm still laughing when we join the queue for Gregg's—to get a cupcake I promised Harlow to cheer her up—when the old lady in front of us turns around.

Her entire face lights up, and she presses her hands against my bump. "How cute," she gushes.

I'm frozen for a second, my cheeks burning as I turn to Harlow. She has the same wide-eyed expression as me.

The lady continues touching me. "How far along are you? My

daughter could never give me grandkids. Babies are so precious."

I'm completely speechless. I open my mouth to answer, to order her to get off me, but no words form. I'm not sure if it's the rude behaviour we encountered today or the fact I wasn't in the best of moods to begin with, but I'm at a point where I am going to lose it. When she presses harder, my princess wakes, kicking out at the hand and making me wince. She presses down on my bladder, and I groan.

I'm beyond pissed.

Like, mama bear pissed.

Who in their right mind thinks it's okay to touch women's bumps? A stranger at that. It's like my belly has a sign on it, saying, 'Touch Me'. If you did this to anyone who wasn't pregnant, it would be considered assault.

"Dear, she just kicked," she gushes.

Having had enough, I remark, "Excuse me, could you not—"

My lips tighten when she reaches for her husband's hand, taking him off guard by placing his hand near hers.

"Can you feel it?" she asks him.

"Oh yes, how lovely," he murmurs, beaming up at me.

Harlow snickers beside me, and I narrow my gaze on her. I don't want her encouraging them.

Too late.

"Our daughter could never have grandbabies. We were so disappointed," he tells me, running his hands over me like he has a right.

That's when I snap. I take a step backward. "Well, you're not having mine, so both of you get your paws off my stomach. Now!"

The old woman inhales sharply. "Watch your manners, young lady."

The nerve! "Manners? Where were your manners when you just had your dirty mitts all over my stomach?"

"That is no way to talk to your elders," the man says calmly.

I narrow my gaze on him. "I'm sorry. Would it have been politer if I had started rubbing my hands all over your stomach?" I snap my mouth closed when I realise how that sounded.

Harlow's laughter echoes around us. I squeak and grab her arm, pulling us away from the couple.

"Stop laughing," I warn her. "The nerve of some people. What is it with people today? Have I got something on my back?" I turn around, giving her my back, but don't give her a chance to answer. "I cannot believe she stood there touching me, violating my personal space like she had a right, then acted like I was the one in the wrong. Seriously… Who the hell do they think they are?"

"I don't know, but your face was a picture," she admits, laughing. She holds her phone up, showing me her screen. The picture is of my side profile, and you can see how pissed and shocked I am.

I shrug, not in the least bit offended that she took an unflattering picture of me. "At least I have a picture of her so I can remember who she is. Shit, she freaked me out."

Suddenly, a shiver runs down my spine and the hairs at the nape of my neck stand on end. I scan the area, looking for anything or anyone out of place. I can't get the feeling of being watched off my mind.

"What's wrong?" Harlow asks, coming to a stop next to me.

I shake my head. I'm being silly.

"It's nothing. Come on, let's go get me an outfit for my date, then maybe we can try to brave the queue again without being mauled," I tell her, causing her to giggle.

I give one last look behind me, still feeling eyes on me, but when I see nothing, I shake it off and force myself to smile at Harlow's reply.

———

"Finally," I cheer as we leave the store. I wasn't sure I was going to find clothing that fit that I also liked.

But we did it.

What made it hard was because I wasn't sure where we're going. In the end, I went with dressy but casual. The dress shows more cleavage than I'm usually comfortable with, but I'm just glad I found something I like. Plus, after I've had the baby, my boobs will probably sag, so I'm flaunting it while I have it.

"We've still got an hour or so before Mason picks us up. Should we go for coffee?" Harlow asks, stretching her back.

"Why don't we go to the club and meet Mason there?" I ask, knowing the club is close by.

Harlow nods. "Beats sitting around here waiting."

"What is the club called?" I ask. I never really paid attention before. I know where it is though.

"Malik said it used to be M5C, but Mason changed it to MC5. The rest argued for a while over it."

"Why?"

"Well M and C are their initials, and there is five of them, but Max and Myles said MC5 sounded like a motorcycle gang."

"A motorcycle gang? We have scooter runners, not MC's running around the place," I joke, chuckling.

"That's why Mason ignored them and changed it to MC5. He said M5C didn't go and sounded too much of a mouthful. Then downstairs is called V.I.P."

"Have you ever been?"

She laughs. "You're joking, right? Malik wouldn't dare let me step foot in a strip club."

"What about the normal bar?"

She shrugs. "Oh, I've been in once, but to be honest, Malik doesn't spend much time there."

So it definitely isn't just me who isn't invited there. For a time, I thought maybe Harlow said she wasn't invited either to make me feel better, and that maybe they said no to her going because I was with her.

"I can't wait to see where he works," I admit, smiling. The last time, the others met us outside so we never got chance to go inside.

We head off in the direction of the bar. It's not long before Harlow breaks the silence.

"How are you and Mason getting along?" she asks, a smile teasing her lips.

"We're getting on really good actually. He is so sweet and attentive.

He's changed so much during the time I've been back. But sometimes I miss his flirtatious personality."

"Have you guys… you know?"

"Had sex?" I ask, chuckling. "No, we haven't, and not for my lack of trying either. He wants to. He has a constant boner that shows me how much he wants to, but he doesn't go further than cuddling and kissing."

My voice sounds bitter, even to my own ears, and I have to wince a little. I sound like a bitch.

"So, you're a sexually frustrated pregnant lady with crazy hormones?" she surmises, letting out a giggle.

"Yeah," I admit, exhaling.

We come to a stop outside the bar, and I look up to the huge sign that has MC5 written in bold red lettering.

"Let's see if we can sneak up on them," I tell her, before pushing open the door.

When we step inside, we rush over to a high table, which is covered by a wooden block. Hiding behind it, we both peek around the side, but my amusement vanishes at what we find.

A girl wearing the club's uniform is leaning against Mason, her fake tits rubbing his arm as her finger runs over his bicep. Mason, who is pouring a pint, doesn't even pay her attention, and I'm not sure if that should bother me. I'm glad he isn't encouraging her, but his silence and ignorance isn't exactly discouraging her either.

I move away from the table, clutching a hand to my chest, and look to Harlow. "That fucking bitch," I whisper-yell. I go to confront them, but Harlow grips my wrist and pulls me back. "Let me go."

"Shush, look," she argues, pointing over to the bar.

A tear slips free, but I do as she says. Mason is no longer masking his indifference. His relaxed expression has morphed into one of annoyance and anger.

His jaw clenches as he turns sharply to the girl. He says something to her before moving to serve someone else.

Just when I think he's done the right thing, she presses her arse into his groin, rubbing herself against my guy.

"That fucking bastard," I whisper, not having the strength to walk away or avert my eyes. I'm about to plead with Harlow to take me home, but then he slams down the customer's drink on the bar and turns a furious glare on the girl, who is now looking white as a ghost.

"I've got a fucking girlfriend. A *pregnant* girlfriend, who I've told you I'm happily in a relationship with," he bites out, punctuating each word.

My heart races at his declaration. He didn't just tell her he had a girlfriend, but that we're happy. Up until now, I didn't realise I feared he wasn't.

"Why would you want to settle down? Why would you want a brat that will end up hating you for running out on it and it's mum in years to come? You aren't fooling me, Mase, or anyone here. I know you'll have those pants of yours down at your ankles by the end of the week."

Unable to take it anymore, I step out from my hiding spot, and this time, Harlow doesn't stop me. Instead, she follows behind me as I walk up to the bar.

Mason doesn't see me at first. He's too busy giving Fake Boobs her last warning, but when he turns to talk to the customer he was in the middle of serving, he stops and meets my gaze. If I hadn't just witnessed their encounter for myself, I'd say he had something to feel guilty about, even though he doesn't. It's me who feels guilty. I doubted him. For a moment, I doubted his words, and now I feel like shit.

"Babe," he calls out, and the girl working behind the bar swings her attention to us.

When her gaze lands on me, I give her a little smirk before heading over to Mason. "Hey, baby," I coo. "We wanted to run by and see you in action. Is it okay if we wait until you've finished?"

He smirks at my deviance, and leans over the bar to press a kiss to my lips. "Always. Grab a chair and I'll be over. I just need to finish serving."

I nod and watch him leave to take a food order. I'm entranced for a moment, watching his fine arse strutting into the back. I'm so lost in a dream that I don't see the bitch in front of me until she clears her throat.

I tilt my head up, giving her a fake smile. "Hi, I'm Denny; Mason's *girlfriend.*"

Her gaze holds pity, even as a smirk tugs at her lips. "Well, enjoy it while it lasts."

I tilt my head to the side, pouting. "Why do you say that?"

"Because Mason doesn't do girlfriends. He does fuck buddies or one-night stands."

I inhale dramatically. "He doesn't? I guess you'd know from experience, right?"

Her smirk spreads, like she truly thinks she hurt me. "Not yet, but I will."

I lose the façade and turn to Harlow, snorting. "Did you hear her?"

Harlow nods, a twinkle in her eye. "I did."

I turn back to the girl, leaning in further. "Trust me, sweetie, you'll be waiting an awfully long time for that to happen. He's with me and that's how it's staying."

She scoffs, shaking her head in pity. "Because you're carrying his sprog? Sorry, *sweetie,* but you're probably not the first girl who's tried to tie him down. Once he sees what a mistake he's made, I'll be here waiting."

"Are you sure about that?"

"Oh yeah," she declares, her eyes narrowed on me.

I pat her hand, and she shoves it back out of reach. "You seriously are delusional. Everything about me is real; everything he sees in me is real. It's me he comes home to, me he shares a bed and a home with, and it will be me who marries his sorry arse. Now I expect you to get off your high horse, realise what a slut you sound like, and fuck off."

"You need to hear what you sound like. I'd bet my whole month's wages that the baby ends up not even being his."

She didn't just go there.

"Well, unlike you, I can keep my legs closed. Did you ever think that he only slept around because none of you were ever fucking worth more? He knew he could never take you home to meet his